DEVIL'S GONNA GET HIM

The New  tery

"TAMAR...
SMART,...

"THE SUCCESSFUL FIRST NOVELIST RETURNS
WITH AN EQUALLY STRONG SECOND EFFORT . . .
Wesley has crafted another intriguing plot showcasing
the appealing Tamara, one of the few
women of color in contemporary mysteries."

Booklist

"WESLEY'S ENTRY TO THE FIELD
ADDS A WELCOME NEW VOICE AND
A FRESH POINT OF VIEW."

USA Today

"POWERFUL . . . ATMOSPHERIC . . .
SHARP-WITTED"

Publishers Weekly

"IN A WORLD FILLED WITH
MYSTERY WRITERS, WESLEY IS IN
A CLASS ALL HER OWN.
She is definitely an author worth reading."

Allentown Call

"I SEE A FLOURISHING CAREER
FOR TAMARA HAYLE.
She has a way with a wisecrack
that is positively lethal."

Washington Post Book World

Other Avon Books by
Valerie Wilson Wesley

WHEN DEATH COMES STEALING

VALERIE WILSON WESLEY

DEVIL'S GONNA GET HIM

A TAMARA HAYLE MYSTERY

AVON BOOKS ◆ NEW YORK

AVON BOOKS
A division of
The Hearst Corporation
1350 Avenue of the Americas
New York, New York 10019

First Avon Books Printing: June 1996

AVON TRADEMARK REG. U.S. PAT. OFF. AND IN OTHER COUNTRIES, MARCA REGISTRADA, HECHO EN U.S.A.

Printed in the U.S.A.

RA   10   9   8   7   6   5   4   3   2   1

For my father, Bertram W. Wilson, who has always honored writers.

I'd like to thank Faith H. Childs and Stacy Creamer for their support and encouragement; P. I. Audrey Moore; Janis Spurlock-McLendon, M.S.W.; Lt. Alex Bearfield, Ed McCampbell, M.D., and Lawrence Robinson, M.D., for their expertise; the Essence crew and friends: J. Cain, G. Chambers, J. Nelson, J. Nash, P. Hawkins-Bond, B. Little-Virgin, R. Robotham, L. Villarosa for their cheers, and as always my husband, Richard, for his love.

Devil's gonna get you
Devil's gonna get you
Devil's gonna get you
The way you carryin' on.

Porter Grainger

1

"**S**o you're Tamara Hayle," said the tall, gaunt man who walked into my office without knocking. "DeLorca says you're the best P.I. in Essex County. I only do business with the best." He had flawless dark skin, thick silver-gray hair, and was dressed like a banker in a navy pin-striped suit and black wing-tipped shoes. But he had the dead eyes of a street thug. *Killer's eyes*, I thought to myself, even though I knew better.

Lincoln E. Storey was a legend in Newark, and I wondered why the photos that always ran in *Black Enterprise* and on the business pages of the *Star-Ledger* never captured the predatory glint in his eyes. I also wondered why DeLorca, chief of the Belvington Heights Police Force and my grumpy ex-boss, had given me such a sparkling endorsement.

"Yes, I'm Tamara Hayle. Would you like to sit down?" I asked, extending a hand. He

1

glanced at my offering but didn't take it. I reached for his overcoat, a dove-gray cashmere number that felt as soft as mink against my palm, and hung it up on the rocky coat rack in a dark corner of my office.

"I assume you know who I am," he said with an arrogant thrust of his chin.

"Is there anyone in the state of New Jersey who doesn't?" I hated the ingratiating sound of my voice, but it was too late to call it back. "What can I do for you, Mr. Storey?" I asked, trying hard to tone down my eagerness.

"I'll get to that," he snapped in a way that told me he was a man who was used to taking his own time and getting his own way. His tone caught me short, but I tossed him a sugary smile, deciding in that instant to listen to my pocketbook rather than my pride.

For "the best P.I. in Essex County," I was broke as hell. With a 1982 diesel Jetta that needed a new transmission and a big-mouthed teenage son to feed, being anything but pleasant to the biggest client who had ever graced my funky little office would be just plain foolish.

Spring had touched everything in Newark but me. The cherry trees were blossoming in Weequahic and Branch Brook Parks, and folks, sick and tired of the hawk and the harshest winter in fifteen years, were stepping out into the sun. My best friend Annie had fallen in love with her husband of the last ten years ... again. After the worst year of his young life, my son Jamal had beaten down grief and discovered, with a vengeance, the opposite sex. And Wyvetta Green, the owner of Jan's Beauty Biscuit, the beauty salon downstairs, who I could always count on for her sweet spirit and sour words, had dyed her hair a hot-to-trot blond and was planning a week in Jamaica with her gold-toothed boyfriend Earl. But I was horny *and* broke, and I couldn't think of two worse things to be in spring which, up until this year, had always been my best season. It didn't bode well for the rest of the year. I'd been sitting at my desk, lamenting my sorry state, when Lincoln E. Storey had walked through my door. I wasn't about to let him walk out.

"Could I get you something to drink, Mr. Storey?" I asked. "A cup of tea?"

"I don't drink tea."

"How about some coffee?"

"Freshly brewed?"

"Sorry, I don't have a pot. Instant okay?" I asked. I don't like instant, but I keep it in my office to be polite.

"I don't drink that shit."

That "shit" business threw me for a minute, but I swallowed the urge to tell him to kiss my behind and watched him as he crossed his long legs and surveyed, I feared, the secondhand computer that separated us, the film on the window that dimmed the sun, and the

3

streak of brown gravy that had found its way to the front of my blouse, when I'd shared some egg foo yung with Wyvetta for lunch. I also recalled the first time I'd seen him.

I'd been twelve years old then, one of maybe three hundred bored kids assembled in our junior-high auditorium to honor him on Black Heroes Day. Lincoln E. Storey, a local boy made good, had grown up on the mean streets of the toughest ward in Newark and made money's mama as one of the first black investment bankers on Wall Street. He was, as the principal told us in a flowery introduction, a young man who had studied hard, paid his dues and made his dreams come true.

This was the late 1960s, a time for dreams— and nightmares, too. The flames of the riot in '67 had charred the city's soul as hard as burnt wood. Everybody was looking for a hero, and Storey was made to order. He was in his twenties then, old by junior-high standards. He'd stood tall and stern in his charcoal gray suit and explained the market and how he'd learned to work it, and how if we studied hard, we could learn to work it, too. We didn't understand the market, but we understood rich and the reverent posturing of our principal and teachers, who gathered like spring hens around a young cock.

But later that night when I'd mentioned Storey to my father, his eyes had darkened.

4

"I remember Lincoln, Seafus Storey's boy," he'd said. "He lived in that dilapidated old tenement over there on Irvine Turner Boulevard, just off Avon, back in the days when Turner Boulevard was Belmont, before the big-time Negroes took over City Hall. His daddy used to whip that boy all up and down the avenue every time the mood hit him good. I always wondered what became of him."

I remembered my father's eyes as I watched Storey now and wondered how old he had been when the cruel lines around his mouth had settled in his face as deeply as dimples.

"How long have you been in this business?" Storey asked, snapping me from my memories.

"Five years going on six."

"You're licensed by the state?"

"Of course."

"What kind of things do you handle?"

"Anything that comes my way. Disappearances. Missing persons. Occasionally the Public Defenders will ask me to help on a homicide or larceny. Insurance fraud."

"And your rates?"

"Depends on the job, plus all my expenses."

"And you're worth the money?"

"That's what they tell me."

"Do you find this line of work hard for a woman, a black woman?"

"No harder than being a cop."

"You used to work for DeLorca, I take it."

"Six years ago."

"Why did you leave?"

"I got sick of it," I said, wondering how much DeLorca had told him about me.

"Sick of . . ."

"Sick of being called a nigger bitch by my brethren in blue every day of my beat," I said, the old anger surfacing again, coloring the edge of my words. Storey chuckled deep in his throat, and our eyes locked for a moment, telling me he hadn't forgotten his roots. "So I take it you live in Belvington Heights?" I asked, knowing the answer but tired of answering his questions.

"You grew up around here?" he asked, changing the subject. His thin hand swept elegantly toward the window indicating that "around here" meant East Orange, Newark, and beyond.

"East Orange. Newark. The same ward as you."

A glint of something I couldn't read came and left his eyes.

"Discretion means as much to me as money," he said, out of nowhere.

"I know how to keep my mouth shut."

"You do surveillance work?"

"I've done it."

"You like it?"

"It depends."

"On?"

6

"On who I'm following and where they lead me."

He smiled a crooked smile that told me nothing. "I need to get some . . . information on somebody." He paused. "I need to know every bit of shit about this motherfucking cocksucker that I can possibly get. Do you understand me?"

It wasn't the words that got me. I've heard men curse before; my dead brother Johnny could belt them out harder than anybody I ever knew. But the way Storey's face broke when he spoke, the way he lost control and his lower lip trembled and his eyes squinted, was downright scary. Whoever the "motherfucking cocksucker" was, he had made Storey's shit-list big time.

"Is this person an employee?" I asked neutrally, cooling my voice against the heat I heard in his.

Storey smirked. "You could say that, I guess, depending upon how you define employee."

He was being cagey, and I wondered why he wasn't giving it to me straight.

"I take it this is somebody who has betrayed your trust?" I asked, stating the obvious.

"I want to know where he sleeps and who he fucks," he answered bluntly.

"Does he sleep with someone you know?" I asked innocently, making my voice sound

7

caring, sister-gentle, willing to share a brother's pain. *Somebody you sleep with?* I didn't ask.

He straightened his back, uncrossed his legs, folded his hands. "My stepdaughter," he said after a minute. "I assume they're sleeping together. My stepdaughter Alexa is involved with this person, this character. I don't trust him. I suspect he likes my money more than he likes my stepdaughter, and I want to find out everything I can about him."

"So what's his name?"

"Brandon Pike."

"Brandon Pike," I repeated the name once softly, to myself, like I'd never heard it before, but it had hit me like a fast, hard punch in the gut—lower, because when I had known and loved him, that was where Brandon Pike had hurt me: my female center, the most vulnerable part of me.

Lincoln Storey studied my face, taking in the change that I knew was there.

"You know him, then?" He watched my eyes as they dropped. I forced them back up, confronting his.

"Years ago . . . Not well."

Storey seemed to buy it. "He has been seeing Alexa for about a year. She's twenty-three. Dropped out of school in upstate New York. Vassar. Trying to 'find' herself. He's, how old would you say? Thirty-something? He's come into her life. After my money, anyone can tell that. She's got nothing to offer him. He's that kind of man. My wife Daphne and I are very concerned." His eyes sought mine for a reaction, and then he continued. "If I can get something on him, I can confront her with it. It's clear she has nothing to give him."

What is he giving her? I asked myself because that had been Brandon's special talent, giving women what they thought they needed.

I had spent the years after our "affair" trying to figure him out. And all I really knew in the end was that I'd left my joke of a marriage to my ex, DeWayne Curtis, with my head high, and Brandon Pike had brought it low, lower than I'd ever let it fall for any man again.

"I want you to follow him. Find out what you can on him. See what he's up to. Report it to me," Storey continued.

I wondered for a moment if getting into Brandon's business was really an ethical thing for me to do. Was it right to use my professional skills to get even with somebody who had done me wrong? P.I.s are supposed to be objective, removed from the subject. Cool, detached. I wondered if I could be that way where Brandon Pike was concerned. But it had been three years since he'd left me—me wondering what I'd done wrong and if I'd failed him. He'd severed everything then. Professionally. Personally. Permanently.

And ethics aside, I truly needed the money.

And on the real tip, the son of a bitch deserved it.

"What can you tell me about him now? I'll need a recent photo, current home address, work address?" I asked, slipping into my professional mode again, pushing back the personal.

Storey looked at me blankly.

"I know that he got an award a couple of years ago for *Slangin' Rock*, the documentary he did on kids dealing cocaine. Is he making any money yet? Is he still doing docs?"

"I thought you didn't know him well."

"I haven't seen him in about five years," I said, looking Storey in the eye. *Three years.*

"Do you have a recent photo?" I asked again. Maybe he *had* changed in three years.

"Why the hell would I carry around a photograph of Brandon Pike?"

"Why the hell would you come to my office wanting me to tail somebody and not have a picture of him?" I snapped back, deciding in that flash of a moment that maybe I didn't need Lincoln Storey's money after all, not bad enough anyway to put up with his bad attitude. Not bad enough maybe to rake up the embers of Brandon Pike.

Storey smiled what he probably thought was a charming smile. "I like a woman with spirit," he said.

"Mr. Storey, don't waste my time." Suddenly I was as sick of him as I'd ever been of anybody in my life.

"No. To answer your question, I don't have any photographs. And I can't tell you a lot about him because I don't know anything or I wouldn't be hiring you. But I'm giving a fund-raiser tonight, for Stella Pharr. Stella Pharr."

"Tonight?"

"Yes, for Stella Pharr," he said, repeating the name for the third time.

"Stella Pharr?" I asked. I'd heard the name before but couldn't place it. Storey certainly seemed to relish the sound of it.

"Yes. Deputy District Attorney. She's running for state assembly. Alexa, my wife, Daphne, Pike. They'll all be there. At Tate's. You know Tate's used to be on West Market, now it's on Fullbright in Belvington Heights."

"Yes, I know the place." Jackson Tate's ancient, elfin face quickly came to mind. Tate's had been the hottest new restaurant in the comeback of Newark. Tate had raised hackles and eyebrows all over town when he'd moved it to Belvington Heights, which needed another ritzy restaurant like another Lexus dealership. My friend Jake, who loves Newark more than anyone else I know, had been particularly pissed off, despite the fact that he'd briefly worked for Tate as a maître d' when he was in law school and loved Tate's apple pie as much as I did. He hadn't eaten in the new location since it had opened.

Jackson Tate had grown to manhood with my father on Howard Street, a cobblestoned stretch of rowhouses, when it was one of the saddest streets in town. It's all gone now, along with the despair that marked it. I remembered the birthday cakes Tate used to make me and his rolls, "floating light" my daddy used to call them, and I remembered Tate's dream of starting a restaurant: A young man's fantasy come true in old age. But I'd only been to Tate's once since he'd moved to Belvington Heights; his price range was definitely out of mine.

"How much are the tickets?" I asked, wondering if I had the price of entry.

"Two hundred and fifty dollars apiece, but you won't have to pay," Storey said, as if he were reading my mind. "Bring a friend if you want. I'll tell Tate to bill me. I own him."

"You own Tate?" I asked, not disguising the surprised disgust in my voice.

But Storey didn't seem to hear it. He reached into his suit pocket, took out an ivory-colored card with his name and address on it, then a checkbook and scribbled out a check. I glanced at the card and then stuffed it and the check into the slot meant for credit cards in my worn gray wallet, my heart skipping a beat as I noticed the one and three loopy zeros scratched with the tip of his Mont Blanc fountain pen.

"Under no circumstances do I want my wife or stepdaughter to know anything about all this." He paused. "For obvious reasons."

"Obvious reasons?" I could understand his stepdaughter but not his wife.

"Clearly the less Alexa knows, the less she'll share with Pike. I don't want to worry Daphne. She has enough on her mind as is." His eyes shifted away from mine. I wondered if he was lying. Even if he was, I decided it wasn't my business.

"Okay," I said. "As I said before, I know how to keep my mouth shut."

"Get to Tate's before nine. There may not be too much of a crowd then, and you won't have any trouble finding us. Watch Pike carefully. See who he talks to, watch what he does. I'll see you tonight?" he asked, suddenly anxious.

I glanced at my watch. It was four-thirty, but the bank was open late today so I figured I'd have time to scoot by there, deposit the check, and pick up a pizza at Pizza Hut for Jamal before he cleaned out the refrigerator. I'd also call Annie and see if she could pull herself away from William long enough to hang out at Tate's tonight. I figured she would. She liked good food almost as much as she liked her old man, and Tate's still had some of the best food in Essex County.

"Tonight is fine," I said, smiling my sweet, professional smile. But two peripheral questions lingered in my mind: How had Storey gotten a piece of Tate and did I *really* want to know who Brandon was sleeping with? I let them rest, though. Storey's check was already burning a hole in my pocket. "Thank you, Mr. Storey," I said.

"I think we can do business together, Ms. Hayle."

As he reached for his coat off the rack and turned to leave, a sharp, hard rap on the door drew the attention of us both.

"You in there, Tamara?" It was Wyvetta, jiggling the knob on my door. "I still got some of those egg rolls left over from lunch if you want to take them home to Jamal."

"Wyvetta, I have somebody in here with me. A client!" I added firmly, but not quickly enough to head her off. Wyvetta, grinning and waving a greasy bag from the Golden Dragon, barged through the door.

"Oh, girl, I'm sorry . . ." she said as soon as she spotted Lincoln Storey, but just as quickly the smile dropped from her face.

Storey, with a look that could have turned hell cold, stepped away from both of us, his eyes darting nervously to Wyvetta, then back to me, and finally settling on Wyvetta. "Please excuse me, ladies," he sputtered, sweeping his dove-gray coat over his shoulders and

14

nearly knocking me over in his rush to get out the door.

"Wyvetta, do you know—"

"Yeah, I know him," Wyvetta said, cutting me off, her eyes filled with contempt. "I know him better than he thinks." She spat twice, like a cat, in the path Storey had cut, and her spit spread in a thin, nasty line down the hallway that he'd just left.

2

"**W**hat the hell was that all about?" I asked Wyvetta as soon as Lincoln Storey was down the stairs good. She screwed her mouth up into a kid's pout and shifted her eyes to stare at the wall behind me. "You've got to say something, Wyvetta," I said. "You can't just spit at a man like Lincoln Storey and not tell somebody why you did it."

"I can if it's not somebody's business," she said quietly, her brows furrowing and a frown forming on her thin, brown face.

"But to spit at the man, Wyvetta. I know he's nasty, but to *spit* at the man." The line of spit streaked across the hall floor seemed meaner than a string of shouted "motherfuckers" or a slap across the face, and my curiosity was definitely getting the better of me.

"If you don't start using some Ultra Sheen conditioner on those split ends of yours, I won't be responsible next time you sit your tired behind down in my chair," Wyvetta finally replied, leaving *no* doubt that she *seriously* didn't want my nose in her affairs. I tossed her a smile of surrender and let it lay.

Wyvetta and I aren't get-down-to-the-dirt, nitty-gritty friends like me and Annie or some of the other sisters who've been with me through the kind of things it hurts to remember. We're working friends who share lunch or a drink when we feel like it as well as a common mailbox. The little I know about her she's told me in throwaway cracks or moments of mutual intimacy that she assumed I'd forget ten minutes after she'd shared them. But I don't forget much that people tell me. I know that she named her beauty shop, Jan's Beauty Biscuit, after her mother, Jan, who died when she turned eighteen. My own mother died when I hit fifteen, and those early deaths were the first thing we knew we had in common, even though the legacy they left us is different: The memory of her mother nurtures her while mine haunts me. The Beauty Biscuit is also a tribute to Wyvetta's favorite food. My girl loves herself some biscuits—Popeye's, KFC's, the ones you stir up quick with a cup of milk and Bisquick, and the smack-your-mama-in-the-mouth kind your grandma made from scratch. I also know Wyvetta is a hardworking sister who pulled herself up by boot strings when there weren't any boots, the kind of woman who won't ask a favor unless the devil will be paid if she doesn't get it.

Her father was a good-hearted loser smart enough to put his dead wife's insurance money in a savings account, dumb enough to end up in Rahway for killing some fool in a bar fight the year after she died. Wyvetta didn't touch that insurance money until she hit thirty-two (after it had accrued some *serious* interest), and then she used it as a down-payment on the Biscuit, which she's had for about-eight years.

Wyvetta can be as tough as week-old turkey if the situation calls for it, but she's got a tender side, too, especially for her sister Tasha, twenty-three, whom she calls Baby Sister and raised after her parents left the scene. Tasha, who was a sickly child and Wyvetta's only kin, has never wanted for anything; and even as late as last year Wyvetta put up part of the money for her to start her own catering business.

But raising a child before her time has taken its toll on Wyvetta. There's a world-weariness about her that she hides behind her wisecracks and smart mouth. I've always figured her hairstyles—those Marge Simpson beehives she sports, the short, red shag cuts that deck her head every other August, the tight, plastic-looking curls streaked with gold that come out just before Christmas, and this latest blond job—are expressions of that plain old-fashioned foolishness she missed during her teenage years, years she gave to Tasha, who folks say has a wild side, a girl who can turn evil as a goose if you cross her.

I was truly curious about Wyvetta and Lincoln Storey and the ugly bond that made her spit—and him get hat—but I respected her too much to push her any harder, so I let it drop. By the time we got downstairs, my mind was racing through all the things I had to do before I made it to Tate's by eight.

My first stop was the bank where I deposited Storey's check and cringed when my sad-ass bank balance danced in double digits on the ATM screen, and then the pizza shop, where it seemed like everybody in Essex County had decided to cop themselves a slice. It was going on six-thirty by the time I got home and on seven after I'd actually showered and done something with my hair.

My son Jamal came in as I was standing in the mirror putting on my finishing touches— a touch of blusher and year-old lipstick that I dug out of the case with a broken lipstick brush.

"Hey, Ma, what's up?" he asked, chewing on a slice of pizza as he sprawled his lanky teenage frame across the top of my bed, coming dangerously close to getting tomato sauce on my pillow. He had on a pair of oversized jeans, which hung loose around his narrow

19

behind, and a sweatshirt that looked too big and bulky for his skinny frame. His newly acquired "look" was one of studied sloppiness—de rigueur, it seems, for hip-hop stars and teenage boys. His Timberland boots (which I'd bought him for his last birthday, spending more money than I'd spent on myself for a pair of what my friend Annie calls "please-fuck-me" pumps I'd worn to a New Year's Eve party she'd thrown last year) were unlaced at the top. In the last couple of months, Jamal had adapted a slightly roguish, male teenage style that I wasn't completely comfortable with. Black men carry the weight of other people's meanness, and I was always afraid that some fool would judge my son by some thug whose mug he'd just seen on the six o'clock news. But my good friend Jake, whom I increasingly turn to for explanations of Jamal's coming-into-black-manhood changes, had assured me that this adaptation of toughness is a natural part of his finding his identity. Besides, the real deal is that when it comes to the way America judges the brothers, even a Brooks Brothers suit and Coach briefcase didn't count for shit. More often than not, a black male is viewed as a felon no matter what he puts on, so I should just let the boy dress the way he wanted to.

"Going out?" Jamal asked, as he took another bite of his pizza slice.

"Yeah," I said, applying blusher to my right cheek.

"Where you going?"

"Tate's."

"Who you going with?"

"None of your business."

"Working on a case, huh?" Jamal asked with a sly grin. He knew as well as I did how dull my social life had become. If I were actually going on a date, especially to Tate's, he'd have heard about it days ago. I ignored him.

"Don't worry, Ma," he quipped as he came over to peck me on the cheek. "Things will pick up for you, just give it some time. Look at me. Six months ago—just a boring, depressed geek. Now"—he looked over his shoulder at himself in the mirror and blew himself a kiss—"women calling all the time, asking me to the movies, lining up for my phone number, trying to sit next to me in algebra class. Check me out, Ma, the maiden's daydream!"

"Maiden's daydream? Who told you that?"

"None of your business," he responded with a hammy grin. I rolled my eyes, but had to admit to myself how handsome he had become in the last couple of months. And he was right about the girls. They were calling all the time, a development that had definitely begun to pluck my nerves.

"Don't be riding too high, Jamal. Women

don't like vain, self-centered men who are in love with themselves," I said, expressing *my* preference in men more than that of adolescent girls.

"Ma, do I really sound like a vain, self-centered fool who is in love with himself?" he asked quickly, his eyes suddenly wide. I was always amazed just how sensitive Jamal was and how easily an off-hand, critical look or comment from me—even tossed in jest— could shake his self-confidence.

"No, son. Not foolish, just a little vain."

He came over to the chest of drawers where I was standing and sniffed the air, picked up the bottle of Norell that I had just put down, then glanced over at the heap of clothes that were sprawled across the bottom of my bed.

"So what happened to the junk from the Body Shop you always use? Too good for dewberry these days? And speaking of vain, Ma"—he said with an exaggerated nod over toward the heap of dresses that were strewn across my bed in a bright assortment of textures and styles—"you're really going through the rags, huh. So what you working on?"

"You know I can't discuss that," I said with a self-important edge.

"Right, Ma. But don't be looking and smelling too good. Men don't like vain, self-centered women in love with themselves," he added with a mischievous chuckle as he got up, still chomping on his pizza, and lumbered out of the room.

"Just do those dishes in that sink after you finish studying for that chemistry test!" I yelled out, but as I glanced over at the pile of dresses, ranging from a work-a-day gray suit to a slinky red satin number, a wave of self-disgust swept me.

Was it because of Brandon Pike?

I checked myself out again in the full-length mirror I'd hung last summer and wondered again if the black silk suit that I'd finally settled on was right. It was a rich-girl suit, I decided as I surveyed myself in the mirror. Black-woman-on-the-move suit—elegant and undeniably professional. The kind women wore to the affairs I'd once gone to with Brandon Pike. Before he dumped me. The kind girls like me who grew up in the projects in the Central Ward, whose daddies worked in paint factories, whose mamas did day work, aren't supposed to own. A suit for the grown-up daughters of the women my mother used to work for—the rich little black girls whose mothers gave me their cast-off clothes. (And quiet as it's kept, I was always glad to get those fit-for-Sunday dresses—except when I could see the envy in my girlfriends' eyes when I wore them, and knew I was a fraud.)

I don't belong here.

That was how I'd felt when I'd gone out

with Brandon to those parties, fund-raisers, and the cozy suppers to woo his patrons.

I don't belong with people who can afford $250 dollars a throw just to be in each other's faces. People who could finance the documentary films that Brandon made.

"It's a rich man's art. You see all those rich brats in film school, don't have talent worth pee, but daddy is bankrolling, that's what blows my mind, Tamara," he had told me one morning. I'd just brought him coffee in bed (my good Jamaican Blue Mountain), something I will never do in life again for any man.

"And this is the way you make the contacts for your grants and fellowships and the rest of the bucks you need for your films?" I'd asked sweetly. "These one-hundred-fifty-dollar parties and the rest of the stuff you drag me to?" I'd added with a girlish giggle tacked to the end of the sentence. (You'd think that after DeWayne Curtis, my ne'er-do-well first husband, I'd have tucked that act where the sun don't shine, but as my grandma used to say, a hard head *do* make a soft behind.)

"You know you like it," Brandon teased. "You're the kind of woman who deserves to go to four-hundred-dollar parties and drink good champagne."

"The champagne ... yeah," I'd said. He'd laughed, but then his eyes had left mine and went to a place mine couldn't follow.

"You win some shit, like I did last night,

24

and people pay just to hear you talk. You flatter a few rich assholes, charm their stupid wives . . ."

"Stupid wives!" I'd exclaimed, offended in the name of female solidarity. I'd pulled away puzzled, glimpsing for a moment something that I'd never seen before, which disappeared as quickly as it came. His eyes turned back to mine.

"Yeah. The ones who brag about how their mamas used to pass for white at Lord and Taylor's forty years ago, the ones who drop a couple of grand at Bergdorf's every spring."

"You sound cold, Brandon." The tone of his voice, the look in his eyes, had chilled me, but not enough—I'm ashamed to admit—to throw him out of my bed.

"This business is all about networking, Tamara. And I network with any rich nigger who can turn me on to any richer white boy who ain't afraid his lady's going to want my dick. Networking, money, and charm, baby. Because the bottom line, Tamara, is I'm an ambitious son of a bitch who's going places. Want to come along for the ride?"

He'd pulled me over to him then and kissed me so tenderly I would have gone almost anywhere in the world with him because he was unlike any man I'd ever known. He had ushered me into a rich black world that I'd only heard my mother talk about, and when I was with him, for the first time in my life I felt comfortable around people whose houses she'd cleaned.

I'd seen Brandon Pike only once since that morning, and I hadn't thought I ever would again. But now there was Tate's. And the world I'd entered and left on his arm. Lincoln Storey's world. Brandon Pike had hit the motherlode, I thought ruefully, giving my rich-girl suit one last glance in the mirror, and I was on my way to see just how deeply he would dig.

3

Belvington Heights, the town where I was headed, where I used to be a cop, is separated from the city of my birth by race, money, and sixteen miles north on the Garden State Parkway. As I shifted the Blue Demon (Jamal's nickname for our car) into second gear and climbed the hill that divides Belvington Heights—"the Heights" as it's called by the natives—from the rest of the world, I turned my thoughts to the business at hand: the sticky problem of tailing Brandon Pike.

It's easy to follow somebody who doesn't know you from nothing, especially if you're black and a woman. The world takes you for granted then, and you're always somebody's something else—sister-lady ringing up the groceries or sweeping up the floor. I do my best work when people are limited by their own expectations. I smile a lot. Flash my toothiest grin. I've even been known to bend my head slightly and nod a bit to the left. A pleasant young Negress. A dependable, unassuming presence. And while I'm doing my act, I can follow some all-assuming fool to the ends of the earth, making all the notes I please. I love it when they realize that all the while I was bowing and scraping I was steadily kicking ass.

But that pose wouldn't work with Brandon Pike for obvious reasons, and if I hadn't been so eager to kiss Storey's butt, I'd have told him that it would have been wiser to follow Brandon from a distance, using what we call in the business a stationary tactic: long-range observations with a good pair of field glasses and zoom lens for the ancient Nikon I inherited from my brother Johnny. I knew my usual surveillance modus operandi—adding a couple of pounds via an old sweatsuit of Jamal's, a gray wig courtesy of Wyvetta, and glasses I'd picked up at Duane Reade—wouldn't work. It would be smarter, I decided, to tail Alexa for a day or two, avoiding Brandon altogether until I got a sense of how much time they were actually spending together. Since Storey had hired me to tail his stepdaughter's lover, he probably wouldn't object to a further violation of her privacy.

As for tonight, I'd be direct when I spotted Brandon. Seeing him for the first time in three years, I'd deliver a pert little shout of delight. He was vain enough to believe that a woman he'd dropped like a spoiled tomato would actually be glad to see him again. I'd also let it slip that I'd been invited by Annie, the only sister I knew who could actually afford to come to a party like this. Or better still, I'd let Annie spread the disinformation. As I was pulling into the parking lot, I spotted her red baby Mercedes pulling in behind me.

"So what's up, sister?" she said, grinning as she looked me up and down as she got out of her car. "I haven't seen you in this one since you wore it with those please-you-know-what-me pumps to my party last year. Who you putting the moves on, and why am I here?"

"Annie, don't start with me again about those damn shoes." She smiled broadly and then stepped backwards to check out her reflection in her car's sideview mirror.

"Do I look alright?" she asked like an insecure kid, sucking in her stomach and standing up straighter. "Does this thing fit okay?"

"You look fine, girl," I said and gave her a little hug to reassure her. She was dressed in a stylish black crepe dress that gently draped her voluptuous body. A string of pearls, a birthday gift from her mother when she turned eighteen, was strewn around her neck in a double strand.

"Mama's pearls?"

"Why not?" she replied with a little shrug. "I know this thing must be big time, 'sweetie.

At Tate's. Mistuh Tate's," she added, lifting her head slightly and exaggerating Tate's name. "Who's it for?"

"Stella Pharr."

"Stella Pharr, very interesting." Annie tilted her head to the side in a caricature of a cartoon detective. "Isn't she that sister who's running for the seat Tilly Dixon had before he got indicted? If she's jamming at Tate's in 'The Heights,' she's got a good stab at it. Who's paying the bill?"

"Don't know," I said with a shrug.

"Right."

"Annie, will you do me a favor?"

"Depends, sweetie," she answered, pursing her mouth like an indulgent grandma.

"Say you invited me loud and wrong to anyone who is listening. Kind of spread the word."

"Loud and wrong? That ain't hardly my style, Tamara. Too, too tacky. I don't know. You know I've got too much class and taste for that kind of shit."

"Right, baby, you and I both know where you keep that good taste hid."

"No class," Annie replied, shaking her head in disgust.

"Tell me something I don't already know. I need this, Annie. It's business. Next month's rent is riding on it."

"Business?"

"Believe me, it's important."

"Sure, no problem," she said finally. "So how much did you say these tickets cost, since I bought them and all?"

"Two fifty."

"As in two hundred and fifty dollars apiece? As in, I paid five hundred bucks for our little brown butts, or big brown butt in my case, to be filling a chair at Tate's tonight?" she asked, her voice rising.

I nodded.

"Let's just pray this loud and wrong mess doesn't reach William's ears, because I know he'll think that I have lost my natural mind."

"You can tell him the truth."

"On second thought, maybe we shouldn't go *that* far," Annie said with a funny little grin. "As long as we've been married, him thinking that I've actually lost my mind for a couple of minutes will probably be good for his hormones. Give me that exciting edge. Add some spice to the old stew. Keep the old dick dicking."

"Annie!"

"Heh, heh, heh, heh," she cackled mischievously like the Wicked Witch from the West, and we headed into Tate's, giggling like teenagers.

When it had been in Newark, Tate's had been an intimate, homey spot, with sepia-colored photos of black folks in Newark in the 1930s and 1940s. The voices of Bessie and Billie lamenting the trials of two-timing poppas had floated from the ancient sound system. Tate's had single-handedly uplifted a desolate corner of West Market Street that everybody but the most dogged believers in the city had written off. In its heyday, it had been the site of many a high-school graduation supper, and dinner for two had become the coveted prize in countless church raffles. Its popularity with New York City journalists rivaled even that of the Portuguese places in the Ironbound, and Tate himself had actually been featured in *New Jersey Style*, a magazine about the "good life" that never ran pictures of any black people. Six months after Tate's left Newark, the old place had been boarded up, and naysayers had one more thing to hold against the city: "Told you this place wasn't worth shit ... Too good for them fools over here ... Can't make no money in a town like this ..."

Newark folks took Tate's departure personally.

But my man Jackson Tate could still rock them pots, and even though the gingery scent of his peach cobbler now mingled with the rarefied air of the Heights, folks still crept back to grease despite themselves, some folks anyway.

Tate was a man who valued a dollar above limb and loyalty, and the dollars were no longer in the town where he'd made his name. But I could remember the burnt brown

32

sugar taste of the caramel cakes he'd always made me for my birthdays. He'd been my father's cut-buddy, his closest friend and drinking partner, always handy with a Kennedy half dollar to pull from behind my left ear and a bottle of Jack Daniels for my folks on Christmas Eve. So I always cut him some slack when folks started talking bad about him. I thought about that now as I walked into his new place.

"Ooomp, oomph, oomph. The Negroes are out tonight," Annie observed with a little jiggle of her hips as we headed to the tables laden with food after the maître d' named "Minnie," weave piled high, tendrils dangling over her hazel eyes compliments of her green-tinted contact lens, had finally found our names on the ten-page guest list.

I glanced around, surprised again by just how much Tate's had changed. Stark abstract expressionist paintings had replaced the vintage photos, and Kenny G. had knocked out Bessie and Billie. The walls in the long narrow room were the color of curdled cream, and each tiny bleached oak table was surrounded by a banquette in plush ocher velvet.

"This is what I call a mix-and-money crowd." Annie glanced at the people who were standing, scheming, and schmoozing. "Ever wonder how money smells, Tamara? Take a whiff!"

Money didn't have a smell, but it had a

look, and you could definitely see it tonight. From the Rolexes that gleamed on strong ebony wrists to the furs strewn casually over brown and tan shoulders, money echoed in the bursts of laughter erupting from the circles of Brooks Brothers men and in the proud looks tossed by their thin, stylish women.

"I knew I should have worn my mink," Annie muttered as she glanced around the room. "I didn't know there were so many rich black folks living in New Jersey." She scooped some guacamole onto a blue flour tortilla chip with one hand and grabbed a glass of champagne offered by a roaming waiter with the other. "Why do we always dip into somebody else's culture when we want to make some cash?" she asked with a disdainful nip at the tortilla chip she was holding. "Why are they doing a Mexican thing? You'd think they'd be doing some fried chicken and black-eyed peas, that's what Tate is famous for."

"Was famous for," I mumbled dryly, dipping a large chip into a spicy bean dip and searching the crowd for Storey and Brandon.

"Oh well, may as well do some networking before all these beans start working on me," Annie said as she gave an elaborate wave to somebody across the room. "Ooooh, I think I knew that hussy at Howard! Hold on to this table, girl, my feet will be kicking my butt in about an hour and I'm going to want to sit down."

I grabbed a glass of wine from a stern-faced waiter. As I sat down, I spotted Jackson Tate talking to a well-dressed faux blonde across the room. When his eyes caught mine, he smiled, excused himself quickly, and headed in my direction.

Jackson Tate had always been plump, but now in his seventies he'd turned those extra pounds into muscle. He looked like he could be hauling furniture instead of baking pies. His broad face was framed by silky hair that was nearly white now but had once been as dark and slick as Billy Eckstein's. There were two things about Jackson that hadn't changed, though: He still called me "Puddin' " and he liked to wink at me, as if the two of us were sharing some delightful secret.

"Puddin'!" he called out. "Tamara. Tamara Hayle. Baby girl, you don't know how many memories you bring back." He gave me a rib-crushing hug, proving his regular workouts in the gym. "Got quite a crowd, don't I?"

"Somebody's going to make a lot of money," I said neutrally.

"So are you part of 'Folks for Pharr'?"

"Is that what they call themselves?"

"That's what Mr. Storey's been calling them."

"*Mister* Storey? I thought you all were partners?" Storey hadn't exactly said that, but I wanted to give Jackson the benefit of a doubt.

"You might say that or you might not." An elusive reply. "You want to see something nice? Come on, Puddin', let me show you my new kitchen. We just put the finishing touches on it."

"New kitchen? Now? In the middle of all this?"

"Come on," Jackson begged, grabbing my arm. "It's so fine, it makes me 'shamed of that hot old hell hole I used to cook in back in Newark."

"You did some serious cooking back in that hot old hell hole."

"Yeah, I guess I did, didn't I." If he looked wistful for an instant, his face picked up the next moment. "Come on." He steered me through the crowd. I followed behind. Judging by the urgency of his grip on my elbow, I figured he had more than his new kitchen in mind. Tate wanted to tell me something in private away from this crowd. I gave the room one more quick look before following Tate through a swinging door at the back of the restaurant.

I blinked in the sudden glare, courtesy of track lighting. Lincoln Storey and a woman in navy were huddled together, talking in animated whispers at a small round table at the far end of the room. As we approached, they glanced up, startled. The woman snatched her hand from Lincoln's wrist. Lincoln, looking through me, then glared at Tate with a scowl.

"Excuse me, Mr. Storey. I didn't know you-'all were in here." Jackson's obsequious tone caught me short. I tossed him a surprised glance, which he didn't notice.

"No problem," Storey said, quickly stretching his lips into a thin, unconvincing smile. "Just going over my introduction with Ms. Pharr." They both stood at once, seemingly eager to end this encounter.

"You've met Stella Pharr," Storey said to Tate, with a nod in her direction.

"I've had the great, great pleasure," Jackson said, with nauseating courtliness as he took both her hands between his. "I'd like you both to meet Tamara Hayle if you haven't met yet," he said with a glance toward Storey. I wondered if he knew that Storey was paying for my supper. Storey ignored the remark. Stella extended her hand toward mine.

She was a striking woman, nearly the same height as Lincoln. Her smile was polite, perfunctory—a distraction while her darting eyes hungrily took in everything they could. The double whammy of her pointed chin and coal-black hair, pulled to the back of her head in a scalp-tingling French twist hardened the beauty that might otherwise have graced her features. Her expensive navy suit clearly spoke business and the gold earrings and thin-chained bracelet that dangled from her wrist did nothing to cut the severity of her look.

Seeing her clearly now, I realized that Jake had introduced us at a party given by the District Attorney's office several months ago. Jake had been there with his wife, Phyllis, and when we'd met, she'd looked me over, her cold eyes trying to figure out my relationship to Jake. Those eyes pierced me now, trying to figure out my connection to Storey.

"I think we met before at the retirement party for Thomas Winsome. Jake Richards introduced us," I said, clearing things up for her.

"Ah, yes," she said, her lips pulling tightly together into what I assumed she meant to be a smile. "You're a cop."

"Was."

Her eyebrow arched ever so slightly. She seemed poised for a question when an armload of trays hit the floor on our side of the swinging door with a deafening clatter.

"Fuck!" squealed the bearer of the trays, spotting the four of us. "Oh fuck," she mumbled again, as she stooped to pick up the mess at her feet. Lincoln Storey and Stella Pharr stepped back and stared at her as if she'd just peed on the floor. The girl looked up again. She did a double-take, as if seeing me clearly for the first time. She dropped everything again and rushed over to plant a big sloppy kiss on my cheek. "Tamara!" she screamed like an enthusiastic kid. "How are you?"

"What are *you* doing here?" It was Tasha Green, Wyvetta's baby sister. I was as surprised to see her as she was to see me.

"Catering, girlfriend!" she said, tossing her head back with a laugh that seemed unnaturally loud. She slid the trays she was still holding onto one of the tables with more force than was necessary. "Now you can tell my big sister, whose always minding my business, that I really am going to pay her back."

Tasha Green had a little girl's infectious good spirits that always brought a smile to my lips. She was a small-boned, petite woman with what Wyvetta called a "gameen" haircut that surrounded her pretty brown face like a curly black helmet. She'd never fully outgrown the frail health that had haunted her childhood. Only last year, during a particularly tough bout of illness, Wyvetta had decided to confide in me: Tasha suffered from sickle-cell anemia, a hereditary form of anemia in which the red blood cells are fragile and shaped like sickles. But there was a healthy bronze glow to her deep brown skin tonight, and I was relieved to see that she'd put on some weight. Her voice, as rich and deep as Tina Turner's, always made me think she was going to break into a chorus of *Proud Mary*.

"Good evening, everyone." Tasha seemed

to be addressing Lincoln and Stella in a far more composed manner as she stepped back from the jumble of trays at her feet.

Lincoln retreated from the silver-plated mess with a studied "I-don't-speak-to-the-help" look on his face. Stella ignored her, too.

"I said, 'Good evening, everyone,' " Tasha repeated, clearly determined not to be ignored. She stared at them both with a look that gave her face a hard edge I'd never seen before. It definitely got their attention.

"How are things going out there?" Jackson asked as he bent to pick up the rest of the trays. Although his tone was pleasant, he threw Tasha a look of rebuke that made her suck her teeth, cut her eyes, and strut to the refrigerator on the other side of the room, opening it with so much force I thought she'd break the spring on the door.

"Time to meet your public," Storey stage-whispered to Stella as he took her elbow and ushered her out of the room. Stella, saying nothing, threw a tight smile at Tasha's back and left the room without looking at anyone else.

"Tough cookie," I said to Jackson when they were out of the room.

"You don't know the half of it," Tasha muttered loudly from across the room.

"Need some help?" Jackson asked Tasha gently. He picked up the trays from the floor where she'd left them and deposited them into the sink.

"Naw, I just came to get some more chips and guacamole." Tasha took a large container out of the refrigerator and banged it down on the table. "I'm going to take this bean dip out now. It has to be room temp or you won't be able to dip it," she added over her shoulder to Jackson, her voice strained.

"You okay?"

"Okay as I'm going to be."

"You want to go home and let me finish up?"

"No. I got to get used to that kind of shit."

"Nobody should have to get used to that kind of shit."

"You have."

"So what did he do to *you*?" I asked Tasha, breaking into their dialogue. Both of them looked at me like I'd just dropped in from Teaneck.

"Have you talked to my sister recently?" Tasha answered me with an amused question of her own.

"Something you want to talk about?" I probed, trying to read the strange mix of sardonic amusement and pain in her brown eyes.

"Not really." She shoved a tray onto the table, loading it with guacamole and chips.

"Why?"

"You'll find out soon enough," she said with a mysterious smirk as she left the room.

41

"How about you?" I turned to Jackson.

"Nothing to talk about."

"How did he end up owning you?"

"He doesn't own me."

"That's what he's saying."

"When did he say that?"

"Well. He didn't exactly say it." I lied; it was exactly what he'd said.

"Where did you hear it?"

"Around."

"Around my ass."

"You act like he owns you. The way you were kissing his butt." I was suddenly angry, for Jackson, for Tasha, for the way Storey had treated them both.

"Was it that obvious?" He said it so pathetically it made me wish I hadn't called him on it.

"What's Tasha got against him?"

"Ask her. I don't tell her business."

"What's he got on you?"

"What's he got on everybody."

"Jackson, how did you let this happen? How did he end up owning your restaurant? He said it, Jackson, *he* said it to my face!"

"Doesn't the devil always get his due?" he asked grimly.

"Well, it *is* a nice kitchen." There was nowhere else to take it, and I realized in a moment of self-realization that I'd deposited Storey's check into my sorry-ass bank account the same as everybody else. I served at his pleasure, too.

"Yeah, Puddin', that it is. That it is."

And it was. Copper pots and antique glass added an elegant accent to the long, brightly lit counterspace. It was the kind of place that would never look messy, even though the dirty trays that Tasha had dropped off earlier shared the yellow and white tiled counter space with neatly lined up bottles of olive and vegetable oils, two jars of mayonnaise, three of peanut butter, sweet and sour pickles, and fresh supplies of tortilla chips and bean dip.

"So Tasha works for you now?" I asked, lightening things up.

"She does the parties I don't want to do."

"And you didn't want to do this one?"

"He don't tell me what I can do in my own kitchen yet," Tate mumbled with an anger that I knew Storey had never seen. "I better get on out there," he said with resignation. "But why are you here," he added, suddenly confronting me as the two of us left the kitchen. "You talking about what he's got on me, what's he got on you? I know you can't be paying good money to be up in these people's faces."

I paused for a moment, trying to come up with something that wouldn't compromise my professional integrity. Maybe Jackson didn't know I was on Storey's payroll after all. "He owes me a favor," I finally said.

Jackson chuckled like he knew I was lying. "Lincoln Storey has never owed anyone a favor in his life."

Annie brushed past us then, just in time. "Hi, Mr. Tate," she said politely. "Make sure you visit the john," she whispered in my ear. "He must have spent a good five thou on the tiles and mirrors alone."

"Six thou," Jackson said, overhearing her. "A good six thousand."

"And somebody's soul?" I muttered bitchily, then, when I saw his face, I wished like hell that I hadn't.

"That, too, I guess. Don't be too hard on me, Puddin', not until you've walked down Bergen Street in these shoes. But don't play me cheap," he said with a wink. "This old boy's got some aces up his sleeve that the best sharks on Prince Street couldn't bluff, and the game ain't over till the last hand's been played." Annie gave us a puzzled look, and then her gaze darted to the front of the restaurant, where a party of three had just entered.

"Girl, isn't that the fool you used to . . ." but before she could finish, I'd turned around to see Brandon Pike, sweet young thing on his arm, strolling into the room like he owned it.

4

Brandon Pike had once told me that women always smiled at him, their good wishes sending him on his way. He walked into Tate's tonight on a wave of female admiration, smiling seductively at nobody in particular. I was amused as I watched him, amazed at how little things had changed. Brandon had always had an unshakable sense of entitlement to the kindness of women.

He was an uncommonly good-looking brother, I had to give him that. Lithe and muscular like a pro football wide receiver, he filled any space he was put into with grace and confidence. Tonight, he was dressed in a three-piece, gray pin-striped suit—Giorgio Armani, I assumed. His skin, a deep brown, was as smooth as a baby's belly, and his hair was cut shorter than when I'd known him, almost to his scalp, like a warrior or gladiator. His angular face was strong, never cute. But his eyes were what got you—haunting eyes that spoke of delight between the sheets. Eyes that could pierce your soul if you let him get that close.

Those eyes got big when they spotted me. Surprise, alarm, I wasn't sure which, probably the latter. I held his gaze for a moment, just for the hell of it, emptying my face of any expression, and then I grinned. A fake, silly grin and shaped his name with my lips: *Brandon, Brandon, how are you?* He smiled with relief, then turned to the young woman who held his arm so tightly she creased his suit.

Alexa Storey looked younger than her twenty-three years, and her body had a girlish coming-into-womanhood plumpness about it. Her long, dark chestnut hair was parted in the middle and piled on top of her head. She was dressed in a burgundy silk dress that had cost somebody some bucks but that was poorly chosen: the style, an Empire-look with long sleeves edged with lace that nearly covered her wrists, made her look matronly, and the reddish hue drained all color from her face. Small pitted scars on her cheeks and forehead hinted that she'd lost a bout with adolescent acne. There was an awkwardness about the way she moved, and a fearful uncertainty in her large hazel eyes. Those eyes followed Brandon's gaze across the room, but there was no malice in them when she caught him returning my fake smile. A quick but uncertain any-friend-of-Brandon's-is-a-friend-of-mine grin flashed on her lips.

A woman I took at first glance for Alexa's older sister followed behind them as they swept into the room. But then I realized she must be Daphne, Alexa's mother. Lincoln Storey's wife. She was the same height as Alexa but leaner, firmer, and I realized with a twinge of envy that I'd seen the black silk dress that draped her size-4 body at a boutique in the Short Hills Mall for a high, three-figures price. Her only piece of jewelry was a solitaire diamond ring on her left hand about the size of a tiny bird's egg. Her smile was sincere and sweet like Alexa's, but her eyes were direct, her almond skin flawless, and her hair a shade or two lighter than her daughter's, courtesy of L'Oreal, I told myself with self-indulgent cattiness. She was the kind of woman that I disliked on sight.

Lincoln Storey, swiveling his head to smile and murmuring greetings to those in his wake, oiled his way through the crowd to reach his family. Holding Daphne's hand, he led the three of them back toward their reserved spot at the edge of the room with so much silken charm I felt like throwing up.

"That is him, isn't it?" Annie asked anxiously.

"Lincoln Storey?"

"No, fool! Brandon Pike."

"Yeah, it's him."

"I thought I heard the sound of panties dropping all over the room!"

"Well, you must have heard your own because mine are firmly on my behind."

"He's certainly come up in the world. God, I can't wait to tell my mother that I saw him with Alexa Storey, Jewel's granddaughter. Daphne Winston Samson Storey is Jewel Winston's daughter. My mother hates Jewel Winston."

"Hates her? Why?"

A tall, cheerful waiter waltzed by with a tray of champagne. Annie grabbed a glass and took a fast gulp.

"You know mama's a big club woman, or at least she was before her stroke. Anyway, Jewel Winston, Missus Dr. Daniel J. Winston, Daphne's mother, blackballed mama when she tried to get into the old Negro Ladies' Culture Circle in the fifties. Said she was too dark. Mama doesn't forget stuff like that. She still gets mad talking about it."

"Too dark? Thank God we're finally past those days." I shook my head in disgust.

Annie looked at me in amazement. "Sweetie, where have you been? Don't you watch those videos? If girlfriend's black, she looks like Kate Moss with a weave, tits, and a tan.

"Anyway, color was very big in Daphne's family, and they made no secret of it. They came up from Atlanta in the forties. One of

East Orange's oldest richest Negro families. Old tired Negro doctor money, thank you. Mama always said she thought they were a little bit weird, a little strange with their colorstruck selves. That was all the women did, mama said, preen about their pretty selves, their money, and their color. Mama claimed the doctor only treated folks who passed the paper bag test."

"Paper bag test? I haven't heard anybody mention that since grandma died." A vision of my wise, funny grandma came to mind.

During one of our talks about what ailed the world, she'd told me that once upon a time, if you were darker than a paper bag, you couldn't get into certain "respectable colored" establishments or marry into certain families. "Paper bag?" I'd asked, incredulous, and we'd both broke out laughing, though her laughter was tinged with a hearty bitterness.

My grandfather was dead by the time I was born, but grandma still talked bad about his people. I remembered their ancient, sepia-colored wedding picture, grandma's skin the deepest, prettiest brown I'd ever seen against his, the color of cream. His family had been mad because he'd married "too dark," but that was before my father, their first pretty little brown grandbaby, came along. Then all bets were off.

One Thanksgiving when I'd been a kid with all my uncles and cousins and aunts crammed into grandma's tiny place, I'd arranged nuts in a dish by their color. "This looks like us," they tell me I'd said. "Yeah, a bunch of nuts," wisecracking Johnny added. Everybody laughed then because there were so many shades of brown, tan, and cream in our family. I didn't like to think that that particular slice of American racism had hurt our family—other things but not color.

"Mama liked to died laughing when Daphne's first husband, Alexander Samson, kicked the bucket and didn't leave her a pot to pee in. Mama does have her edge," Annie continued, bringing me back to the present.

"When Daphne got married, the man looked like he might have some money. He was a handsome something, at least by her family's standards, but it was all show, no investments. She didn't make that mistake the second time around, and as far as Jewel Winston was concerned, Lincoln Storey's bank account definitely Europeanized those African genes."

I glanced over to Storey's table at Daphne and Alexa and then at Brandon.

The ones who like to brag about how their mothers used to pass for white at Lord and Taylor's.

But that had been Daphne's mother a long time ago.

Tasha came by with a phony smile pasted on her face and a tray of food: a silver bowl of guacamole surrounded by chips, and strips of broiled chicken on toothpicks. Annie and I grabbed as much as we could without looking tacky. I had another glass of wine, and we sat down across from one another at one of the tiny tables.

"This is something, isn't it?" Annie said, looking around the room as she sipped her champagne. "This is the real stuff, too," she added with a glance of admiration at the glass. "But whoever is paying for all this better leave some money for the campaign."

I nodded in agreement. "I'm going to go check out that ladies' room you were raving about," I said as I dabbed at my lips with a yellow cocktail napkin. Annie nodded between munches and threw somebody standing at the bar a 14-carat grin.

I glanced into the kitchen as I passed by on the way to the back of the restaurant. Tasha had gone in ahead of me, and the door hadn't swung completely closed yet. I could see her, hand on hip, placing appetizers on a silver tray. She looked tense and distracted as she worked. I thought about saying something— I was still curious as hell about why Wyvetta had spit at Lincoln Storey—but decided it was wiser to let that particular dog stay asleep, especially since I was working for him. And the last thing Tasha needed was me in there bothering her when she was trying to do her job. So I went on my way without saying anything.

Annie was right about the ladies' room. Jackson Tate had gotten a bargain for his six grand. The walls and floor were covered with what looked like hundreds of tiny black tiles; the golden fixtures on the sink shined like the real thing. I primped in front of the gilded mirrors for a couple of minutes, grinning, playing with my hair, spraying cologne from the fancy bottles sitting on the counter, even pumping a squirt of Caswell Massey lotion onto my hands from the bottle that sat beside the cologne. I promised myself that I would have to bite the bullet and bring Jamal here for his next birthday; but I knew that once he saw this place Red Lobster would be history.

I ducked into one of the stalls, and then sat down, got back up and sat back down on the toilet seat several times trying to figure out how it knew when to flush by itself. I was finally ready to leave when I heard two women come in through the outer door. I stayed put.

"Why won't you listen to me, Alexa?" said Daphne Storey. "Why won't you just listen to me?"

There's nowhere like a public bathroom for overhearing intimate conversations, so I pulled my feet, scrunching up on the toilet seat so no one could see that I was there. Two high-heeled shoes clicked past my stall, and then someone knocked on the door. I held my breath.

"It's locked, because it's broken," Daphne Storey said irritably. "After all the money Lincoln paid for this damned place, that fool Tate hired some second-rate plumber to fix the toilets, and that one's been flooding ever since, so I told him to keep it locked."

"He told me it wasn't true. I believe him. Why isn't that enough for you?" Alexa said, apparently in response to her mother's question.

"Lincoln says it is, so he's out to destroy him, and you know that he will. There'll be nothing left of him when Lincoln is finished. Why don't you listen to me?"

"Since when in this lifetime have you believed anything that asshole says?"

"Don't talk about your stepfather like that!"

"As if it really mattered a beggar's fuck to you."

"And don't use that kind of language around me. Your mouth is as filthy as a Springfield Avenue whore's."

"Just like my mama's?"

"I should slap your face."

"You think so?"

Someone turned on the water, and I heard it splash as if she were washing her face.

"Do you have any lipstick, Mommy?" Alexa asked. "I forgot mine at home."

"You'd forget your fat ass if it weren't hanging on your back."

It was the little-girl tone that shocked me,

53

even more than the mother's ugly, hurtful reply. There was such longing for approval in Alexa's tone and so little of it coming, the disparity tugged my heart. For a moment I had an impulse to cough, kick my foot against the door, do anything not to be privy to the sad bond between these two women. But I knew I couldn't. I had been paid big money to find some truths that involved Alexa. I couldn't blow my cover because I didn't like what I was hearing. The truth of the matter is that what I do for a living usually means digging around in other people's shit, and Lincoln Storey had paid me handsomely for my shovel. So I stayed put, my legs doubled up against my butt, and when they started talking again, I listened.

"Who do you think you're bullshitting? I know why you hate him. You probably just wish you were fucking him yourself."

"How many times have I told you not to talk to me like that."

"Where do you think I learned it?"

"Why do you torture me, Alexa? Everything I have done in my life I've done for you. Do you think it's been easy for me—this and those little tricks you play with your life?"

They were both silent for a minute.

"He's getting ready to toast her. We'd better get out there," Daphne said.

"Why do you put up with it, Mommy?

Why do you let him put you down like this?"
the awkward voice of the kid asked.

"Why do you think?"

"I hate you sometimes, for putting that shit
on me. I hate you!"

"You are the most important thing in my
life, Alexa. You must never forget that. No
matter what you say to me, you must know
you are the most important thing in my life."

"If he leaves me, I'd be better off dead."

"You're as much of a fool as your dead fool
of a father."

I heard the outer door close as one of the
women left the room, and then I heard the
other enter one of the stalls and begin to
weep. And then suddenly she began to kick
the stall door hard, like an angry kid throwing a tantrum. She stopped after a minute or
two and left the bathroom.

Had it been Alexa or Daphne?

I waited and then got up, stretched out my
legs, and walked out, too.

The crowd was bigger now, and I didn't
spot either of the women when I got back to
my table. I searched the room for a moment,
and then gave up. But the words between the
two of them stayed with me, and I thought
about my own mother.

Jamal was about the same age now as I was
when she died, a little younger maybe, but I
could look at him and understand the need
and vulnerability I had felt then. I tell myself

that the memory of my mother's cruelty has been blurred by time, that my memories are worse than the actuality. But when I see the bond between other mothers and their daughters, I know that something profound was missing from ours. Most women revere their mothers. I was never able to, and that knowledge has always brought its own shame. I have never understood why she seemed to hate me so.

My father was the gentle one, my grandmother the one I went to for loving, and I pull strength from her nurturing even now. Rage and brutality mark my memories of my mother. They were in every action she made, every word she spoke.

Knocking the black off. That was what she called it when she beat me, which was often and without mercy. *Knocking the black off,* as if she were determined to go to the center of who I was and erase it.

Her beatings and the words that came with them were laced with such cruelty and bitterness, they drove my sister away and Johnny into the depressions that simmered within him and killed him years later. My father, unable to protect us from his wife, drank to protect himself.

Six months after she died, I wrote three letters telling her I still hated her, that I was alive and she was dead, and that she had not destroyed me. I still have those letters written without shame in the pretentious script of early adolescence. I'm not sure what they represent to me, why I've held on to them, because despite her cruelty, I loved her deeply. I have never solved the mystery of my mother, what drove her to be who she was, what meanness in her own past crippled her life. I just know there is a hole in me because of her, and I'm not sure if I can ever forgive that.

Mommy.

Alexa's voice had brought her back and I felt numb and angry as I always did whenever I thought about her.

"Girl, you look like you've seen a ghost," Annie said, when I sat back down. I nodded to reassure her that there was nothing wrong.

But my thoughts were on my mother when I stood with everybody else to applaud Lincoln Storey and Stella Pharr, and when I glanced at his wife and her daughter, I could see no cracks in their armor.

When it happened, it was so sudden there was no time to say anything. Later, we were left with nothing to do but stand around in sad circles, talking quietly of the stealth of death.

At first, I thought he was having a fit. He stood up abruptly, as straight as if he were going to follow his words of praise for Stella Pharr with some additional witticism, a look of surprise on his face, but then he began to claw and grab at his throat, tearing at his own flesh as if trying to rip something out. With the other hand he began to reach for something or somebody, maybe for Daphne, his wife, but she remained riveted to the spot where she sat, her eyes filled with horror. There were a couple of self-conscious titters from people in the room at first, as if our host was just kidding around to bring the night to a humorous end. But then his lips and face began to swell, turning purple and stretching. Within moments, they seemed to be twice their natural size, his features distorted and ugly like those of a ghoul on a Halloween mask. There was utter silence as he began to wheeze and gasp, both hands now around his throat as if he were choking himself to death. His breaths came short and fast then. Saliva spewed from his mouth, spraying the people sitting close to him. There was one final gasp before he fell over, soiling his pants.

We knew then that Lincoln Storey was dead.

"I guess the party's over," I heard somebody say in either incredible innocence or the most tasteless attempt at gallows humor I'd ever heard in my life.

But he was right.

5

My grandma used to say that the last death always brings back the first. I didn't know what she was talking about until folks around me started dying. *Last death always bring back the first.* She'd say it quietly, murmuring it like a prayer while she peeled apples or washed greens in that beat-up old sink with rust for water we used to have in that cheap old place we lived in. She lived next door, until we moved and she died the following year. Then came everybody else.

Lincoln Storey was my last death, jerking like a dancer high on dexies in his thousand-dollar, three-piece suit. When I think about it now, how quickly it had come, leaving nothing but shit on his pants and sins on his soul, I thought about my mother and how fast she'd gone and the mix of feelings she left behind her. Then I thought about my father who'd passed two years after that, and the

one who damn near took me with him—
Johnny, eating his gun on a summer morning.
The last death always bring back the first.

I was definitely in what my daddy used to
call a blue funk, courtesy of Lincoln Storey, a
funk that lasted all day Saturday into Sunday
morning. I just sat around the house thinking
about my dead family and the general bad
turn of events in my life.

It was raining Sunday morning, which
didn't make things any better. Fortunately
Jamal had gone to spend the weekend with a
friend across town, so he wasn't there to witness my deterioration.

But as I lay in bed listening to the rain hit
my skylight, which had started leaking, anger
gradually replaced my depression as I realized I'd have to climb up on the roof when
the sun came out and caulk up the damn
cracks. And when I finally got up around
noon to fix myself some breakfast, sourness
beat out the anger when I realized I was out
of coffee. It was definitely a coffee-drinking
kind of morning. When I need to cool out
or feel guilty about my caffeine-jones, I drink
herbal tea. But the truth is, I'm a die-hard coffee freak. I need that rush to bring me into
the day. In a crunch, though, strong *caffeinated*
tea with too much sugar will get me over. So
I made myself a cup of Lipton tea, piling four
heaping teaspoons of sugar in it, hoping that

a sugar high would compensate for the lack of caffeine.

The doorbell rang three times before I got up to answer it. It was Wyvetta Green, looking as bad as I felt.

"Girl, what are you doing out on a day like this?" I asked.

She didn't answer at first, she just pushed past me into the room, an odd look on her face and her robin's egg blue plastic raincoat leaving a stream of water behind it. In the five years we'd known each other—laughing together, sharing Chinese food, talking bad about folks who plucked our nerves, I suddenly realized that she'd never once been to my house.

"Come on in," I said unnecessarily as she sank down on the couch. I took her coat, shook some of the water out on the front porch, and hung it up.

"I'm sorry it's so wet."

"Wyvetta, it's raining outside." I noticed then that her hair was weird—weird for Wyvetta anyway. Weird in that it was simple: pulled straight back and fastened with a purple scrunchy right below her hairline. She also seemed to be in the same blouse, lightly smeared with hair oil, that she'd worn when she'd spat at Lincoln Storey on Friday.

"They got my baby sister. They got my baby sister, Tamara."

"Who? Wyvetta, what are you talking about?"

"They got my baby sister, Tamara," she said again as if she hadn't heard me. When she looked at me, her eyes were filled with tears. "That son of a bitch. That disgusting old son of a bitch. I told that girl to stay away from him. I told that girl. But she don't listen to shit. Never ever since she was a baby. She don't listen to shit. Mama, *please* forgive me. Please forgive me!" she begged with such anguish that I sat down beside her and took her hands between mine.

"Wyvetta. What happened? *Who* has Tasha? Did the mob get her? The I.R.S.? Girl, what are you talking about?"

She looked at me and then glanced around the room like she just realized where she was.

"I'm sorry, Tamara," she said. "Me coming around here like this on a Sunday, not calling or nothing. You know that's not like me, but I couldn't think of anyone else to talk to, anyone else to help me."

"Why don't you start from the beginning?"

"They arrested Tasha Friday night for assaulting a police officer and resisting arrest."

"Resisting arrest *and* assault?"

"It was late on Friday night. She called me from the jail, that one call they gave her. She was cleaning up after this affair she had catered. Did you hear about Lincoln Storey?" she suddenly added.

62

"Yeah. I was there, at the party. I saw Tasha that night."

"You were there?"

"Yeah. Never mind about that, just tell me what happened."

"Well, then you know that the son of a bitch is dead. I hate to be talking bad about the dead, Tamara, but he deserved it. Tasha told me the cops came to the restaurant poking around after he died once everybody had left. Tasha was cleaning up. One of them got smart with her, and you know how salty Tasha's mouth can be. She always gives back as good as she gets. She cussed them out and threw a bowl of corn chips at them, and they arrested her. And Tasha thinks they're going to hang that killing on her. Hang Lincoln Storey on her."

"Hang a killing on her? Why would Tasha think that they think she would have anything to do with Lincoln Storey dropping dead?"

"Tasha thinks they're going to say she killed him. Murdered him."

"Murdered him! The man died in front of a room full of people. Died of a heart attack." I paused for a minute, struck suddenly by the fact that I really didn't know why Lincoln Storey had died. "Or a fit. Something natural. Standing up in front of a room full of people. How could Tasha, resisting arrest, have anything to do with killing Lincoln Storey?"

"They say they think he was allergic to something, Tamara. Allergic to some food he ate, something that killed him. Tasha thinks they're going to say she knew he was allergic to what killed him, and she put it in his food to kill him."

"Why would Tasha think something like that? What the heck kind of foolishness is that?"

"They got her in jail."

"Where did they put her?"

"Belvington Heights!"

"Oh, Lord!"

"She heard some of them talking when they brought her in. She heard them say they got somebody who heard her say she was going to kill the man that way, with some food. She heard them cops say that she probably served it like she said she would, and she killed him."

Wyvetta covered her eyes with her hands then, and we sat there together for half a minute while I tried to make sense of everything she'd just told me.

"Did you call a lawyer?"

"They're all closed. She called me so late, I couldn't even get nobody."

"That's the first thing you do," I said. "Get the girl a good lawyer, any kind of lawyer, and next time you talk to her you tell her not to say anything to the cops without her lawyer there. They haven't officially accused her of anything too serious yet, so don't go crazy."

"They will."

"Maybe not."

"They will because that's the way things always go down with the cops. They grab the first person they see when something happens to somebody."

"Get her a lawyer fast. Even if it's just for the assault and resisting arrest charge, get her somebody fast."

Wyvetta was right about that being the way things always go down, but I didn't say it. I'd seen enough in my five years on the force to know how charges can snowball when cops think somebody has dissed them, particularly somebody black. If Tasha had cursed them out and thrown a bowl of chips at them, they probably had the girl *under* the jail. Going to jail because you actually did something serious was usually only half the story when you were black with no bucks, and Tasha was both.

"I don't know any lawyers!" For the first time since I'd known her, I saw fear in Wyvetta's eyes.

"I'll call Jake, and he'll be able to hook you up with somebody good," I said quickly.

"Oh God. Why?" Wyvetta moaned. "Why? With Tasha getting sick, too! She's liable to have some kind of sickle-cell attack sitting up there in jail. That can happen to her. She can't take the same kind of pressures as everybody else. She's not as strong. Tamara, will you help me out?"

"What do you want me to do?"

"Can I hire you, Tamara? Can you find out who really did it?"

"There's nothing to find out, Wyvetta," I said. "She hasn't been accused of anything yet."

"If the man died from something somebody fed him and she was doing the feeding, they're going to think she fed it to him," Wyvetta said more loudly than she probably meant to, staring at me in wonder as if she couldn't understand why I didn't get it.

"Did Tasha have a reason to kill Lincoln Storey, Wyvetta?" I asked, thinking about the way Wyvetta had spat at him on Friday, wondering about the real reason Tasha had acted toward Storey like she had on Friday night.

Wyvetta looked away. "I don't want to say."

"I guess that means she did. You've got to tell me more."

"Tasha's going to have to tell you. I only know what she told me about the man, and that was more than I wanted to hear. I didn't want to hear no more."

"But she had a reason."

"Yeah, she had a reason."

"Wyvetta, that reason is what they're going to use against her."

66

"She's not capable of doing something like that to somebody. And even if she did have a reason, I know she didn't do it. Tamara, will you help her?"

I looked away quickly so she couldn't see the distress in my face. Folks have all kinds of illusions about private investigators; half the time we end up disappointing them, and it usually costs more money than they'd planned for the privilege. As a general rule, I try to avoid working for friends; the ticket is always too high and the results are never worth the ride.

"What are your rates?" She tried to sound calm, like a businesswoman negotiating a deal. "Do you charge by the day, by the hour, by the week?"

"It depends."

"How much? I don't want any cut-rate bullshit. I want the real deal. I want all your attention on it."

"Fifty to seventy-five dollars an hour, depending on the job." I told her straight.

"How much will you charge to find a killer?"

"Wyvetta, if they do accuse Tasha of something serious, which they haven't so far, I'm not going to charge you anything to ask some questions . . ."

"Tamara, you know I believe in covering all my bases, and I believe that what Tasha heard those cops say is what is going to happen. I asked you how much you charge to find a killer?"

"Wyvetta, there's no killer—"

"If the man is dead, and they think he was murdered, then there has to be a killer, and they'll say Tasha is it. I don't want to be caught with my drawers down."

"Wyvetta, you're all worked up over something that hasn't happened yet. You're jumping—"

"I can only pay you forty dollars an hour and I can only pay you for *one* week," she said before I could answer.

"Wyvetta, chances are I won't . . ."

"I will pay you forty dollars an hour for one week plus that ticket to Kingston, Jamaica, I bought from Liberty Travel last month, if you will find out who killed Lincoln Storey so my baby sister won't go to jail for it."

"Wyvetta, I'm not going to take your ticket..."

"I can't pay you your full fee, Tamara. And I have never taken charity in my life. I won't take it from you now. Damn it, Tamara, please help me."

She hunched her shoulders up, then let out a long, sad sigh. "I have worked hard. All my life," she said quietly. "I have worked so hard to bring my mother's memory to something. Tasha is all I have. She's the end of my family, so I've got to take care of her. I knew something bad was going to come of this whole mess. I knew it the minute I laid eyes on Lincoln Storey."

She glanced at me then and looked away as if in shame. "After all that," she said in a harsh, funny little voice, "after all that struggling and saving and trying to make myself up into something, trying to make Tasha up into something, she's going to end up in jail just like my daddy. We're going to end up right back in the shithouse, right back where we started."

"No you're not," I said quietly.

"Why not?" she asked, with a laugh that sounded like a cry.

"Because if they end up saying Tasha killed Lincoln Storey and she didn't, I guess I'll have to find out who really did it," I said quietly.

"Can you do it in a week, Tamara?" she asked. It was more a plea than a question. "In a week?"

"Yeah," I said, with confidence that came from I don't know where. "Or maybe less."

6

The next morning I put on my going-to-meet-the-man gray suit, ate a buttered English muffin, drank a cup of Lipton's mixed with sugar, and went to get the goods on Tasha Green from Roscoe L. DeLorca, chief of the Belvington Heights Police Department. Due to my five years in the department and premature departure, DeLorca and I had, as they say, a "history," so I could usually get in to see him without waiting too long. But when I walked into his hole of an office, which his massive hulk filled like an aging bear penned in a cage at a petting zoo, he tossed me a sinister look.

"I send the man to you as a favor, Hayle. Next thing I know he's dead. Dead. Same goddamn day."

"If you're talking about Lincoln Storey, he hired me as a P.I., not a bodyguard." I shot him a sinister look of my own as I slid into the chair across from him.

70

"Bodyguard, P.I., you're a cop, Hayle, you're supposed to be on top of these things."

"Ex-cop, Chief."

"Once a cop, always a cop."

"So what did he die of?" I asked.

"Allergic reaction to something he ate."

"Isn't that considered a natural cause?"

"Not in this case."

"You think somebody killed him?" I asked, amazed at how accurate Wyvetta's sense of this thing was playing out.

"That's what it looks like. Word's got out on this Lincoln Storey business, and everybody in the whole goddamn state has found out that he didn't die from natural causes. Every son of a bitch who wants to get his name in the paper—from our asshole of a senator to the goddamn leader of the NAACP—wants to know what *I'm* going to do about it."

I nodded my head sympathetically as he exhaled in disgust and gave me what passed for a smile. I decided not to mention that I'd actually been at the scene of death. DeLorca wouldn't waste any time taking a statement from me if he knew I'd been there, and I didn't want to chance ending up being a witness for the prosecution.

"So what can I do for *you* this morning?" he asked.

"I'm working on a case."

"Think you can keep this one off the slab

until lunch?'' He leaned back in his chair with a chortle that ended up as a cough, his jowly cheeks turning an unbecoming shade of pink against his pale blue shirt. ''So what really brings you around here?'' He picked up a cigarette, lit it, looked at it lovingly, then snuffed it out. Nothing about DeLorca ever seemed to change, from his eternal battle with his nicotine jones to his suit.

''Tasha Green.''

''Tasha Green? Oh, Christ! Hayle, is that who you're working for? Her chances of getting out of this one are as dead as Storey. Give it up.''

''You really think Tasha Green did it?''

''We know Tasha Green did it.''

''Well, I guess I'm here to get some facts so I can find out who really killed him then.''

''You're a nice lady, Hayle, and despite what's gone down, I respect your intelligence, but listen, let me save you some time, save you some face. Tasha Green killed Lincoln Storey. First degree, second degree. Let the lawyers fight it out. But we got the cookie dead to right. Tasha did the bean dip and the bean dip did him in.''

''Bean dip?''

''Bean dip.''

''Can I see the report?''

He paused for a minute, considering. ''Knock yourself out,'' he finally said as he shot it to me from behind his desk. ''You're working for her, I'll take your word for it. If it's okay with Tasha Green and her lawyer, it's okay with me. You want to see a copy of the M.E.'s report, too? Here." He shot it across in the same path. "Check it out. It all adds up."

"Got everything sewed up pretty fast, didn't you?" I asked, knowing how long official reports usually take.

"When somebody like Storey dies, it puts fire under everybody's ass, and mine is blazing. Like I said, they want answers. I'm the answerman, and I've got to get them fast."

"And wrong."

"Chair's there if you want to look it over, but read it quick. I got somebody coming in here in fifteen minutes. You owe me one for this, Hayle. I should make you get the info through her lawyer." He nodded toward a slightly soiled brown corduroy chair against the wall. "Be my guest."

I sat down and skimmed the papers. Wyvetta was right: Things did look bad for my girl Tasha.

The reporting officer, somebody named Gilroy, had been called to Tate's at 10:40. When he arrived, he was told by an attending physician, a guest at the "Folks for Pharr" fundraiser, that Lincoln Storey was dead. The doctor had pronounced him officially so at 10:25. He must have been among the half dozen or so guests who had lingered after the gala had come to such an abrupt end. Annie along with me and most everybody else had left soon after we realized that Storey was dead. Death does have a way of clearing a room.

The doctor also said that from the look of the body and what he had observed of Storey's movements before he died, he was sure the man had suffered a severe allergic reaction to something he'd eaten. It looked to the doctor as if he had died of anaphylactic shock, a sudden severe reaction to a substance that a person is allergic to. When asked if her husband was allergic to anything, Daphne Storey, who was crying hysterically the reporting officer noted, said that the only thing that she definitely knew he was allergic to was peanuts, and that as far as she knew he hadn't eaten any that evening. He always avoided any food that even looked like it might have nuts in it, nuts of any kind. When asked if he'd carried a kit with a syringe prefilled with adrenaline, which people with severe allergies carry, she said he always carried one, but it had been used several weeks before when he'd had another allergic reaction, and he hadn't replaced it. After identifying herself as Deputy District Attorney and a close friend of the victim, Stella Pharr had suggested that the officers gather samples of the food on Storey's plate for testing. The reporting officer and the backup had done just that.

At that point, Tasha Green, who was in the

kitchen cleaning up, had been questioned. According to the report, Tasha had "become extremely uncooperative, used abusive language, spat at the reporting officer, and thrown a bowl of tortilla chips." She was subsequently arrested for assault and resisting arrest.

According to an attached statement taken later that evening and to another one taken Saturday afternoon, a witness, whose name had been blacked out by a marker, stated that a month prior to the incident, Tasha had said that "sneaking some peanuts into the old bastard's food" would be a good way for somebody to kill him. She had apparently made this remark after witnessing Storey's severe reaction to a sauce made with peanut oil. Another witness later verified that she'd also heard Tasha make this statement.

There was also a memo attached dated this morning with a short report from the police lab stating that peanut butter had indeed been found in the bean dip. The report had been done on overtime because of a special request put in by the District Attorney's office.

As Wyvetta feared, Tasha was charged with the first-degree murder of Lincoln Storey early this morning.

I handed the thing back to DeLorca, who took it eagerly, glanced at it with a slight smile, and shoved it into a folder.

"What's her motive?"

"Talk to your client. That's all I'm going to say."

"It's a fast hop to arrest Tasha Green for first-degree on the strength of some vague statement from some unidentified witnesses, who for all you know could have motives of their own. Why not the wife, Daphne Storey, for that matter? The spouse is always the first one you haul in when somebody dies an unnatural death."

Annoyance spread across DeLorca's face. "For your information, we've checked into that possibility, and we found it's highly unlikely. She lacked opportunity. And means. What was she going to do, carry the dip in her evening bag and slip it on his chips when he wasn't looking?"

"Why not?"

"District Attorney Stella Pharr, for reasons of her own that will remain her own, was watching the wife like a hawk that night, and she'll testify to the point that Mrs. Storey didn't have the opportunity or the means."

"What about the others? The daughter. Brandon Pike. Exactly what kind of relationship did this Stella Pharr have with Storey?"

"As far as I'm concerned, we got the goods on the one who did it. Motive. Means. Opportunity. That's all you need. Talk to Gilroy. She brought the girl in. Maybe she can give you something else. Don't count on it, though,"

DeLorca muttered, ignoring my questions with a wave of dismissal.

"Gilroy?"

"Matilda Gilroy. Just came in a couple of weeks ago. One of our older rookies." He nodded through his glass window toward my old desk, and I caught sight of an aging blonde sipping coffee out of a Dunkin' Donut paper cup as she wrote something onto a pad. "You all have a lot in common. Maybe you can give her some tips. She reminds me of you," he added with an uncharacteristic sweetness that made me glance up at him in surprise. But he pointedly avoided my eyes, as he cleared his throat and got back to his work.

I went over to talk to Matilda Gilroy and introduced myself, noticing the green box of Sleepytime tea next to the cup of pencils on her desk.

Gilroy was slender and tall with large, calloused hands, a bad complexion, and too much makeup for the job. Each of her large earlobes had been pierced twice, and blond was definitely not her natural color; the dark roots peeking out from her edges made me wonder if Wyvetta ever worked on white women. Her smile was open and quick, and her teeth were slightly bucked. I liked her at once.

"Tamara Hayle, I've heard so much about

you." She put down her pencil and stood to shake my hand.

"Good things, I hope," I said, and we both chuckled. I glanced around her cubicle at a photo of a kid with ringlets for hair and a cherub's face.

"My son, Jeremy," she said following my gaze. "That was taken a few years ago. He's about six now." Besides the fact that we were both female, that was probably what DeLorca meant; he was the same age as Jamal was when I joined the force.

"How are they treating you?"

"As badly as I expected. But I'd been warned. I heard the crap they pulled on you and your kid. It made me sick to my stomach."

"Had the same effect on me, too. I haven't eaten chili since."

"They taught us at the academy that the way to humanize a force is to bring on more women and, you know, more minorities."

"I guess he's doing it a half step every five years."

We shared another laugh, and I wondered for a moment if what we had in common—single motherhood, sons, herbal tea, De-Lorca—could overcome the chasm and discomfort that race always seems to create between people who might otherwise easily become friends. The cop role was familiar to both of us, though, and we slipped back into it quickly.

"I just read the report on Storey and Tasha Green," I said getting right to the point. "It was a good, thorough report. You were the RO on it, right?"

Gilroy's eyebrows raised questioningly, so I added some explanation without going into detail. "I'm working for her sister. Was there anything else that wasn't in the report, anything that you wouldn't mind sharing?"

Gilroy thought for a moment, wondering what, if anything, was appropriate to share just as I would have if I'd been in her shoes.

"Can you tell me a little about food allergies? It seems kind of a strange way for somebody to kill."

She studied me for a moment, probably wondering if she should talk. She gave a backward glance at DeLorca, and then motioned for me to sit down at her desk.

"You know when the witness said that he'd had one before, I knew even before they tested for it that that was how she'd done it," Gilroy said in a hushed voice. "Those kind of fatal food allergies are more common among children than adults, but they are on the rise. My son, Jeremy, is allergic to soybeans, not as severely as Lincoln Storey was allergic to peanuts, but he breaks out in hives. I've got to be real careful. I read somewhere that potentially life-threatening food allergies affect a relatively small percentage of people, about two percent of adults. Lincoln Storey was obviously one of them."

"Did you make any personal observations regarding any of the people assembled, anything like that? I'm trying to figure out if this case is really worth my time. How did the wife act? The kid, the kid's boyfriend?"

"About what you'd expect. The wife was hysterical like I said in the report. Poor woman. I really felt bad for her seeing her old man die like that right in front of her." Her eyes softened for a moment. "She couldn't stop saying his name. The daughter just stared at him; she was probably in shock, and the boyfriend, Brandon something or other . . ."

"Brandon Pike."

"He just looked like he wanted to be somewhere else. I didn't notice anything out of the ordinary about any of them. Just three people caught in a nightmare."

"And Tasha Green?"

Gilroy stiffened slightly. "Tasha Green? A true-to-life little bitch on wheels, if you ask me. Got a temper that's going to get her dead or in jail." Gilroy shrugged. "I guess in a way it already has."

"How do they think she did it?"

"Well, they only just arrested her for it," Gilroy said cautiously, the good cop not wanting to serve an official hypothesis before its time.

"How do *you* think she did it?" I'd never known a cop who didn't have a Monday morning quarterback's take on how the game was played, so I emphasized "you."

"Well," Gilroy said considering, "that's easy enough. She probably just mixed it in there when she made it and made sure he got some of it on his plate. That's not hard for a cook. There've been a couple of cases where people have gotten peanuts or peanut butter in something they don't expect it to be in—food like chili, spaghetti sauce. I remember something a few years ago where a highly allergic college student ate some prize-winning chili that had peanut butter mixed in with it as a thickener, and she died. Peanuts is one of the more common allergens. Tasha Green was just lucky nobody else kicked the bucket. We'd have her on a multiple if they had."

"But isn't that farfetched? Do you mean to tell me neither Storey or anybody else with him couldn't taste the nuts?" I asked, even though, I had to admit, I hadn't myself.

"I don't know if you've ever made bean dip, but I used to make it in the bar I used to work at."

"You worked at a bar?"

"My ex owned one in Harrison. He started knocking me around, so I took the kid and left. Anyway, I used to make bean dip to serve on two-for-one nights. It's almost the same thickness as peanut butter, even the same color. If you hide the nutty taste with a lot of chopped onion, cilantro, and chili pepper, who can tell? People are usually so soused when they're eating it anyway and they're not expecting it, so if they even think they taste it, their minds tell them it's something else."

She was right about that. I'd had more than my share of wine, dip, and everything else that night, and I hadn't noticed any odd flavors in any of it. If I were allergic to peanuts, I'd be laying in the morgue beside Storey.

"Have you talked to Green?" Gilroy asked.

"Have they moved her yet?"

"No, she's still in a holding cell here. We'll be moving her over to county this afternoon if she doesn't make bail, and I don't think she's made it yet."

"Do you mind if I see her?"

Gilroy shrugged. "I don't have any problem with it. I'll call down and tell them you're coming down. You know the way?"

"Some things you never forget."

She turned back to her work, and then glanced up as I was leaving as if she had just remembered something.

"This probably won't mean a damn to you, it probably wouldn't to me if I were doing what you do, but ten years of working in that stinkhole bar of my ex's, I got to know people real good. The tales they tell. The lies they try to get you to believe." She rolled her eyes as if remembering and threw me a knowing smile. "From one good lady-cop to another: Your Tasha Green, she's lying about something. Don't bet next month's rent on this one."

7

"**I**'m glad the greasy son of a bitch is dead," said Tasha Green, nearly echoing the words her sister had spoken Sunday morning. "There's no way they can prove I did it, so they can all kiss my sweet brown behind."

The small, windowless room in which we spoke was hot and stuffy. Belvington Heights, as tight as ever where its hard-working public servants were concerned, hadn't turned on the air conditioner in the building yet, and beads of sweat poked out on Tasha's smooth brown forehead and upper lip. She was wearing the same white catering uniform and apron that she'd had on Friday, but it was wrinkled now and soiled down the front. The smudged black mascara and liner around her big eyes made her face look like a baby racoon's, and she had a slightly sour smell to her, like she needed a bath.

" '*Greasy* son of a bitch?' " I couldn't resist

asking her. "Greasy" was the last word I would have used to describe Lincoln Storey.

"As in slimy."

"You're glad he's dead? Tasha, you're talking pretty tough for somebody sitting in jail accused of killing him," I scolded in a low voice, tossing a sideways glance at the cop with the gray crewcut and Charlie Chaplin mustache who sat in the corner reading a torn copy of *Muscles*.

Tasha glared at the guard. "I don't care if he hears me or not," she said defiantly. The cop acknowledged her stare with a scowl.

"Have you talked to your lawyer yet?"

"I don't want to talk to a lawyer. All I want to do is get out of here."

"When you talk to your lawyer, he'll probably be able to get you out on bail, providing Wyvetta can get hold of some money," I explained gently.

"Probably?" Tasha whined like a kid. "Probably? Tamara, I can't stand it in here. Tell my sister to get me the fuck out of this place. I feel like shit. I'm afraid I'm going to have some kind of sickle-cell crisis stuck in here. A person like me is not supposed to be in jail!"

"Your sister is doing the best she can do. But maybe you should have thought about that before you threw those chips at those cops." I was annoyed at her tone, recalling

Wyvetta's face on Sunday and some of the things folks said about her spoiled baby sister.

But I was worried about Tasha having a crisis, too. I knew that sickle-cell anemia can be very serious without proper medical care. Even though she was talking tough this morning, I couldn't tell by looking at her how strong she really was. I made a mental note to call Jake and see if there was any way we could get her special consideration because of her chronic condition.

Tasha blew a long, tense breath out toward the ceiling. "And I didn't throw those damn chips at those stupid cops anyway. I threw them on the floor."

The cop in the corner folded down the magazine, glanced at me and then at Tasha with a look that said he didn't appreciate the "stupid cops" bit. I gave him one of my sweeter smiles, and he cocked his left eyebrow, looked at his watch, and returned to his magazine.

"Why don't you start from the beginning?"

"What beginning?"

"The beginning of why you're glad the 'greasy son of a bitch' is dead."

"Me and half a dozen other people."

"Let's start with the one who's in jail."

Tasha sucked her teeth loudly, rolled her eyes back up into her head, folded her arms, and glared at a far wall. I remembered Gilroy's words and wondered if maybe I should take her advice. Then I thought about Wyvetta.

"What *is* your problem, girl?" I asked her.

Tasha didn't say anything for a moment, then she sighed. "You think it was the money?" she turned to me and asked like a kid. "Yeah, I think it must have been the money," she answered herself with an affirmative nod. "He wasn't nice. He wasn't really fine. He didn't even fuck very well. It *must* have been the money."

"Money will definitely take you places you don't ordinarily go," I said. "Then you *were* sleeping with him?" I asked quickly, wanting to get that straight.

"Had been." She gave me a smile laced with a snicker.

"How long?"

"On and off? About three years."

"Three years?" I screeched so loudly that the cop cleared his throat and peered at both of us from over the fold in his magazine. "Tasha, three years ago you were barely out of your teens! The man must have been in his early fifties! You were going with a man in his early fifties?"

"I'm not the first young lady to be attracted to older gentlemen," Tasha replied defensively in a mocking tone.

Or their money, I thought but didn't say. "But more than thirty years!"

"I also had, you know, a little thing that really

meant something to me going on the side. But I figured he did, too, with his wife and all," she added with a touch of self-righteousness. "I guess you could say we *all* had a little something on the side."

I shook my head in amazement and wondered if Wyvetta knew everything she thought she did about her baby sister, and just who, between Tasha and Storey, had really seduced whom. But it wasn't my role to judge, I decided in the next minute. My youth had certainly been marked by what some folks kindly call "spirit."

"I take it there wasn't really love between you and Storey, since you had that little something going on the side and all."

"At first there was, not love but like, and then it was just sex, for him anyway."

"And for you?"

"What do you think?" she replied with a bluntness that startled me.

"What did you get from all this? I mean *really* get. Cash? Clothes? Jewels?" I thought about the rock that had sparkled on Daphne Storey's finger Friday night, and my eyes shifted down to Tasha's hands, which save for the bright red polish on her short, well-manicured nails were bare.

"Wyvetta didn't tell you?"

"I wouldn't be asking if she had."

"He put up the other half of the money for

me to start my business, and he paid for my place in University Haven."

"University Haven?"

"Yep," she said brightly.

University Haven was a community of spanking new two- and three-bedroom town-houses in the middle of Newark within skip-ping distance of three major universities: the University of Medicine and Dentistry of New Jersey, the New Jersey Institute of Technol-ogy, and the Newark campus of Rutgers Uni-versity. The stately coops, touted as a key site in the reclamation and rebirth of the city, were just high-priced and classy enough to attract upwardly mobile young buyers who wanted to raise their families in the city.

"I had a *two*-bedroom townhouse," Tasha said wistfully. "It had a dishwasher, a patio, a microwave, a car garage, and everything. But I got thrown out last Thursday. He had the marshal come and throw me out. In front of all my neighbors and shit! Do you believe that? Damn! It was so humiliating! Nobody can get away with humiliating Tasha Green like that!" She gave an exaggerated shiver and shook her head as if trying to erase the memory.

"Do you know why he stopped paying for it?"

"Yeah, I knew. He broke up with me. Said he had found the love of his life again. *Can* you imagine that shit? The fucking 'love of his life *again*.' Like he'd lost her and refound her and shit. That corny-ass son of a bitch! God, I don't know why the hell I ever climbed in bed with that geek!"

"Did he say who it was?"

"Lincoln Storey never told me anything that really meant anything to him. No, he didn't tell me."

"And you have no idea?"

"It could have been his wife for all I know. She was sitting all up under his stupid behind at his table Friday night."

"What about your business?"

"He owned part of that, too. Like a silent partner because of the money he put up. He was just about to call in his chips on that, too, just like my house. But now that he's dead"— a sly little smile formed on her lips—"you know, now that he's dead . . ."

"Now that he's dead, honey, you just might find yourself sassing guards and knitting sweaters for twenty-five years to life if we can't find out who really did this," I said, reminding her of her real situation. The smile quickly slipped from her face.

"Well it's not like I'm the only one who could have done it."

"You're the only one who actually spelled out how it could be done. It's not every day that it would occur to somebody to use peanut butter as a murder weapon."

"Well anybody who had seen him laid out

on the table that night he got that peanut oil would have thought about it."

"The cops say they have a witness who said you threatened his life that night."

"Threatened his life!" She cut her eyes to the ceiling and gestured wildly with her hands. "What are they talking about?"

"Actually, they say that they have two people who say that they heard you describe how you would kill Storey."

"Two! I'll bet one is Minnie, that cheap weave-tossing slut who Lincoln hired as the maître'd'. I'll bet he was doin' that little hoochie on the side. Girl, you can't trust nobody these days. And now she's saying I killed the man! I'll bet . . ."

"Hold it, honey." I held up my hand like a traffic cop. "Calm down, Tasha. Think about it. Tell me who was there and what you said."

"Okay," she sighed and took in a deep breath, as if she were going to do a recitation in a high-school assembly. "It happened about a month ago. We were at Tate's, in the kitchen. Me. Mr. Tate. Minnie the hoochie, Alexa . . ."

"Alexa Storey?" I asked puzzled. "Storey's daughter?"

"His *step*daughter," she quickly reminded me. "That's how I met Lincoln, as a matter of fact, through Alexa."

I drew back in surprise but decided to let it go for now. But they seemed an unlikely match, Tasha Green and Alexa Storey, even though I guessed they were the same age. *Had Storey actually seduced a friend of his young stepdaughter?*

"Where did you know Alexa Storey from?"

"From around," Tasha said evasively. "How is she doing? With all this shit happening, is she okay?" Tasha added anxiously with seeming concern.

"I haven't heard anything one way or the other," I answered truthfully. "You know Brandon Pike, too, then?"

"Yeah, I know him," Tasha said, shifting her eyes from mine.

"Go on," I said, not quite sure what to make of those eyes.

"Anyway, we were all standing around there in the kitchen. Mr. Tate was feeling real down for some reason. Real depressed. I think he was pissed off at Lincoln about something. I've never seen him so mad before. But he wouldn't say why." She glanced up at me, and a mysterious smile suddenly played on her lips, "Why don't you ask Mr. Tate about Lincoln dying like he did."

"Don't worry, I'll talk to him, too. Then what happened?"

"They were all there for dinner. Lincoln, Mrs. Storey, Brandon, Alexa. It was some kind of big-time celebration dinner for some rich white guys and Stella what's-her-name, that tightass old broad who was with him on Friday.

"Anyway, Alexa comes into the kitchen to give back something that belonged to me, but since everybody was there—Mr. Tate and Minnie the hoochie—we couldn't really talk, and right as she was getting ready to leave, Mrs. Storey comes running into the kitchen, screaming about Lincoln passing out or some kind of shit.

"God, it was like the damn restaurant was on fire, the way everybody was running around all of a sudden. I peeked out and Lincoln was laid out on the table shaking like a junkie. Some doctor friend got a needle out of that stupid little kit Lincoln always had on him and gave him a shot of something. And Mrs. Storey was screaming about somebody calling an ambulance, which the hoochie finally did, and then Mrs. S. started yelling at Tate about what he'd put in the food, was he trying to poison her husband and shit, and Mr. Tate finally said that he'd just made this sauce that had been over the chicken, and she asked what was in it and he said peanut oil, and she completely freaked out, saying that Lincoln was allergic to peanuts, seriously allergic."

Tasha, animated by the telling, gave me a strange little smile. I turned to see that the cop in the corner was waiting as anxiously as

I was for the end of the tale. He peered bug-eyed over the top of his magazine.

"And then I just said it. After Mrs. Storey left. I didn't say it in front of her, you know, I didn't know if she knew about me and Lincoln, and I didn't want to rub it in her face."

"What exactly did you say?"

Tasha shrugged. "I was mad at Lincoln, anyway, for something that he'd said to me earlier." Her eyes shifted from mine again. I suspected I wasn't getting the whole story, but I didn't call her on it. "By then I knew he was alright, the doctor had given him that shot. I was *joking*, for Chrissakes, I thought everybody knew that. I just said that if anybody wanted to kill the old bastard all they'd have to do was sneak some peanuts into his food. I didn't mean nothing by it." She looked at me and I could tell she was eager for me to believe her. I wiped all expression from my face.

"Well, now they think you meant something by it."

Tasha sucked her teeth again and shrugged. "Stupid cops," she muttered. But then a look of wild panic crossed her face.

"Tamara, do you really think they could put me in jail for killing Lincoln Storey?" For the first that afternoon I saw the raw fear beneath her fast-talking bravado.

"Honey, you're *already* in jail for killing Lincoln Storey," I said quietly.

Tasha put her hands over her face and began to bawl, and my heart went out to her. I touched her shoulder gently. When she started to shake, I crossed the table so I sat next to her and hugged her like I used to hug Jamal when his world seemed irrevocably broken.

"I'm sorry. I'm sorry," she said to me or the cop or whoever was listening. "Oh God, why am I such a fuck-up? I'm always letting Wyvetta down. She told me to stay away from that man. Why am I such a fuck-up?"

I didn't answer her. I just let her sit there for a couple of minutes, crying, whipping herself for past sins and for the sake of her sister. Finally I cleared my throat and offered her a wrinkled Kleenex from the bottom of my bag, which she used to blow her nose.

"I just wanted to be somebody," she whimpered. "I wanted to make Wyvetta proud of me. She's done so much for me. Lincoln seemed to be the way to do it. He was rich and famous and he was willing to do whatever I asked him, at first. It was really something having him in my corner. He made it so I could go out on my own—my own place, my own business and she didn't have to worry about me. She could do things for herself for a change."

"Then he left you?" I said it as more of a statement than question.

She paused, playing with the Kleenex. "Well, it's really not as easy as all that."

"What do you mean?"

She glanced around the room and then bent over to whisper in my ear, as if suddenly aware of the cop, who by now had dropped his magazine and was openly curious.

"I'm pregnant," she said with a goofy grin. "About two months."

"And it's Lincoln Storey's child?" I asked, knowing the answer and somehow not surprised.

"He claimed it wasn't, but it's his, and I could have proved it with a blood test if I'd had to. Alexa knew I was telling the truth, and she would have called him on it, too."

"A blood test isn't always conclusive if you have a certain blood type, and if you really want to fight it," I said. "But Lincoln Storey's not around now to fight it anymore, is he?"

"No. I guess not." Tasha answered more flippantly than I thought she should have.

"So who was the little something on the side?" She looked up, tears gone, surprise on her face.

"The little something on the side you mentioned earlier."

"I'm not ready to tell you that yet," she said, surprisingly defensive.

"Did that little something on the side know about you and Lincoln?" I asked, staring straight at her.

She stared back.

"Maybe that little something on the side was jealous?" I decided to push it. "Maybe that little something on the side is the reason you're sitting up here in jail?"

Tasha tapped a strange little rhythm on her belly as if she were signalling the child-to-be within her.

"Could that little something on the side be the father of your baby?" I asked more sharply.

"You know who this baby belongs to now that his father is dead?" she said, looking me squarely, defiantly in the eye. "Me, that's who. But it's Lincoln Storey's kid, and no matter what I did to get it, I'm entitled to some of him now, too, just like everybody else."

She stood up then and, with a glance at the cop, left the room without saying another word.

8

I'd be lying if I said that Tasha Green's parting crack hadn't chilled me, and all that eye-cutting and tooth-sucking told me that what folks said about her was probably true: Wyvetta had spoiled the girl rotten. But I wondered if she was guilty of murder or just hot drawers and loose lips.

Mixing peanut butter with bean dip to send somebody into anaphylactic shock seemed a mischievous, childish thing to do. I could almost imagine a kid, mouth fixed in a pout, chuckling to herself, deciding it would be a hell of a practical joke to make Storey look like a fool in a room full of his highfalutin peers. Maybe "the kid" remembered how Storey had flipped and flopped on the table when he'd gotten the peanut oil that first time. Maybe "the kid" had figured that after it was over, after he'd fallen out like a drunken fool, Big, Bad Mister Thing would

get up and walk away, humiliated but chas-
tened—like an actor does on TV after fake
blood is spilled and fake bullets shot. Maybe
death hadn't been in "the kid's" plan, Storey
hadn't died the first time, had he? Could this
have been a dirty trick that ended up as
murder?

*. . . and no matter what I did to get it, I'm
entitled to some of him now, too . . .*

A spoiled brat's words. Winking at death
and the grief it brings. Tasha was definitely a
kid around the edges. I wondered how Wyvetta would take it if Tasha had actually
done it?

Back in the shithouse right where we started.

Wyvetta loved her sister, but she was entitled to the truth—whatever that truth was.
And if it was a hard one, better I tell her now
than she learn it from the cops. Maybe Tasha
could get off without doing too much time if
she was guilty. Juries didn't look kindly on
fifty-year-old married men doing the do with
girls just out of high school, even if they pay
for their sins with their lives. They'd have to
keep Tasha off the stand, though. The girl
would definitely do herself in.

As I wheeled onto the main drag from the
police department, I headed in the direction
of Jackson Tate's place. Whoever had killed
Lincoln Storey had been in Tate's restaurant
the night Lincoln Storey's allergy to peanuts
was revealed. Tate would be able to verify

what Tasha had told me about who was there that night as well as give me the lowdown on Tasha and her thing with Storey. He also might have some dirt on the rest of the crew, maybe even that "little something" Tasha was doing on the side. If he would talk.

The reality is, nobody has to tell a P.I. shit. They do it because you've tricked them into it, or they're playing their own odds, or they just don't give a damn. Everybody has their own endgame, and I wondered if Jackson would feel like sharing his with me—even though we went back, way back.

The day was too damn hot for spring, which told me it was going to be a summer and a half. I rolled down my window, glancing at the dashboard with the broken air conditioner that had given out last August with a cough and a puff, and wondered if I'd have the bucks to fix the thing before the summer heat from hell. Despite my telling Wyvetta that I didn't want to take her money, God knows I was glad she'd offered it. I wanted to send Jamal to a computer camp in upstate New York to keep him off the streets and that was going to cost some bucks. I knew he'd probably wear those hot-ass Timberland boots into next January, but he'd outgrown most of last year's summer clothes—and for that matter so had I, I thought with disgust.

"Damn!" I muttered sourly as I thought about sleeveless dresses, swimming suits, sexy shorts, and wondered if I could scrape up the bucks to join Weight Watchers and renew my expired membership to the YWCA. Maybe I would just go to Sports Authority and get some free weights. I'd seen an article in *Essence* about working out with them. Maybe I'd just eat soup for dinner every night and tack that article up on the wall and work out every morning before I left for work. It wasn't like I had to punch a timeclock.

So my mind was on bucks and my butt as I rolled into Tate's nearly deserted driveway. I didn't see the bronze BMW, pretty as a new penny, that pulled out fast, slamming into the front of the Blue Demon.

"Jesus Christ!" I cursed out loud as I whipped back into my seat. I reached for the door handle, blood pressure over the top, hell-bent on laying into the driver with every variation of motherfucker I could think of. But before I could open my mouth, he stepped out of his car.

It was Brandon Pike. But he looked distracted, almost shaken, like something weighty was hanging on his mind. He was as surprised to see me as I was to see him.

"Tamara Hayle?" he asked as he opened my door like a doorman looking for a moment like he was waiting for a tip. "Tamara? Are you okay?" I got out of my car without answering him, straightened out my take-care-of-business gray suit, and went around to check out the front of my car. "Looks okay to me, nothing's dented," he said, as if trying to encourage me to come to the same conclusion.

I studied him for a minute, my head tilted to the side, an evil-looking-sister scowl on my face.

"Speak to me, woman!" he begged suddenly, his face losing its troubled look as he smiled at me with a charming grin. "Seriously, are you okay? I'm really sorry about that. My mind was definitely not on my wheels. Earth to Tamara . . . baby!" he teased, lifting my chin with the tips of his manicured fingers.

"I'm okay," I said, jerking my head out of his reach with a definite attitude.

He was dressed in jeans that were worn at the knees and generally loose fitting but snug in the places that count. His expensive cable-knit black lamb's wool sweater gave him a look of studied, sloppy elegance. Johnny had once warned me to stay away from men who spent more money on their clothes than I did, and that truth struck me now like a swift kick to the knee cap. When I caught a lingering whiff of the Chanel for Men he always wore, I didn't enjoy the memories it brought back.

"I thought I recognized your car. It's been a while, hasn't it?"

Not long enough.

"What are you doing here? Did you know

he's closed for the week, at least until next Friday, out of respect for Lincoln Storey?"

If somebody drops dead in the middle of your restaurant because of something he ate, that did make good sense, I thought wryly.

"Were you here to see Jackson Tate, too?" I asked pleasantly.

"Business to take care of," he mumbled evasively and a little too quickly. "Why didn't you come over the other night, stop by, say hello. I was hoping we'd get a chance to catch up."

His girlfriend's stepdaddy had dropped dead like a dog in a room full of people, and the only thing this brother could think to ask me was why I hadn't said hello. What was *that* about?

"Well, Brandon, you have feet, too. Why didn't you come over to say something to me?" I asked coyly, not mentioning Storey's death and the obvious. He laughed his rich, seductive laugh. I smiled back.

"That was something Friday night, wasn't it?" The laughter was still on his lips, but as I studied his face a shadow that I couldn't read passed over it. He took out a pair of sunglasses, polished them on the edge of his sweater, and put them on quickly.

"Yes, it was," I said, neutrally, letting it sit for a minute, trying to see his eyes through those shades. "Did you know they're saying he was murdered? They arrested a young woman for it."

"That's what I heard."

"Word travels fast." I played it as close as he did, without the shades. "Docs must be paying pretty good," I added with an admiring glance at his car.

"It's not mine. It belongs to a friend."

"Alexa Storey?"

"A friend," he repeated, as if he hadn't heard me, and his face closed up, telling me I wasn't going to get anything else.

"I saw the doc you got that big award for, *Slangin' Rock?* The one about the baby cocaine dealers." I thought I'd do better to lighten things up. "It was good. Congratulations."

His eyes shifted down at the ground. Was it modesty or something else? "Thanks," he said, as if he meant it. "I didn't know you were into politics. You know, your being at the fund-raiser Friday night. I was surprised to see you there." He was clearly fishing. I wondered what he was looking for.

"I didn't know you were, either."

"You might say I've gotten interested."

I noticed the gold watch that peeked from under the cuff of his black sweater and sparkled as if it were new. His eyes followed mine to the watch and then returned to my face with a look of defiance that challenged me to ask about it.

"You definitely might say that," I said, taking the bait. "That you've gotten interested in politics." He smiled back conspiratorially, as if he appreciated the humor—and I knew he remembered all those times I'd teased him about his "shameless" ambition.

"So you still staying at the same place, same number and everything?" He sounded as if he was getting ready to ask me for a date.

Now that was a curve.

"Yeah," I said puzzled and unable to hide my surprise. "How about you?" I couldn't think of anything else to say.

"Yeah, still got my place on James Street," he said distractedly, but he sounded like he thought I wanted to know.

But I was suddenly annoyed with him, sick of him and whatever game he was running, and it came out in my voice. "Brandon, why the hell after three years—of not answering my phone calls, pretending you didn't know me—would you ask me something like that? I don't care where you live now. Why do you care where I do?" I asked, my voice rising and thick with resentment and hurt that I realized I couldn't conceal.

Damn it! I cursed silently to myself for always being so vulnerable, always so stupidly honest with men I'd slept with.

"Hey." He raised his hands in a mock fighter stance like he was defending himself. "I'm just trying to be friendly and shit. Make conversation. This is uncomfortable for me, too, Tamara. Believe me. I'm embarrassed. I think about us, what went down between us, what didn't go down between us ... What I didn't do ... Should have done ... It was just one of those things, baby. One of those things that doesn't turn out right."

I studied his face for a minute. Wondering what to make of him, what he was up to, why he was here and leaving Tate's so fast that he'd jammed into my car like the devil was chasing him. Then I smiled, calling on the old reserve, getting back my cool.

"Brandon, there are no hard feelings, baby, believe me," I said with a casual chuckle coming weakly from the top of my throat.

"Friends." He held out his hand for me to take.

"Friends," I said with my toothiest grin, and he bent over and gave me a kiss on my cheek. His cologne filled my nostrils.

"If there are any problems with the car, give me a call, you know where to reach me. I know sometimes it takes a while for things to show up on an old model like yours."

"Sure, Brandon. We'll talk again," I couldn't resist saying, knowing I shouldn't tip my hand but doing it anyway.

"I truly look forward to that, Tamara," he said grinning like a lying politician as he slipped into the BMW and drove away in a cloud of dust.

Bastard, I said to myself. *But what had he been doing at Tate's?*

I knocked hard on Jackson Tate's door, still tossing the encounter around in my mind. I knocked again. Maybe Jackson wasn't there; Brandon hadn't definitely said whether he'd talked to him or not. For all I knew, Brandon could have stopped by hoping to catch Tate just as I was; he was driving out fast, mad that he hadn't been there.

Damn. I knocked again, louder.

"Puddin', what you doing out here banging on my door like that?" As he opened the door, Jackson Tate greeted me with the expected wink as he wiped his hands on a dishcloth. He was dressed casually in a pair of slacks and a red cardigan even though he looked like he might have been doing some cooking. "You're lucky you caught me. I've been closed since last Friday. What a tragedy," he said in the same breath, shaking his head from side to side. He stepped aside, and I walked ahead of him into the restaurant.

It was prettier by day than it had been at night. The late afternoon sun played well on the ochre and cream banquettes. The oak parquet floors were polished to a spitting shine. My eyes were pulled over to the spot where Lincoln Storey had died. Jackson touched my hand.

"Don't even think about it," he said gently. "Just don't think about it, Puddin'. I don't know when I've ever seen anything happen as bad as that. I almost feel like closing the place down. Come on into the kitchen, away from here, and have some wine or something."

"I'll have the something. Do you have some tea? Herb tea?" My nerves needed some calming.

"You drink that herbal stuff?" he laughed. "I might just have some of it tucked away somewhere."

I followed him out into the brightly lit kitchen, and we sat down at the small glass table in the dainty black iron chairs where Stella Pharr and Lincoln Storey had sat that night. I wondered who had sat where I was sitting now—Stella or Storey—and thought again about the man and how quickly he had gone. As Tate poured a glass of merlot for himself and turned the gas on under a shiny copper kettle, I tried to remember the kitchen that night.

The counter space was clear now and sparkling clean, but it had been jammed with food that night—bowls of bean dip, jars of Hellmann's mayonnaise, bread and butter, pickles, peanut butter—why the peanut butter besides the obvious?

"I ran into Brandon Pike outside your place. Or rather he ran into me. He was driving so fast he nearly took my front bumper off."

"Are you okay?" he asked with real concern.

I assured him that I was.

"He came by. On some business."

"Something about Alexa Storey?" Jackson looked at me strangely.

"No," he said without telling me what I wanted to know. "Nothing about Alexa Storey."

We sat there for a minute or two in silence as he sipped his wine.

"I think you should know why I was really here Friday night," I said, feeling suddenly like confessing, not lying to this man I'd known all my life. "I was working for Lincoln Storey."

"I figured as much. He had you following Brandon, huh? I guess that job didn't last very long." We both laughed then: gallows laughter that broke the tension. Jackson had a deep, throaty chuckle, the one that I used to hear at night from my bedroom down the hall, the one that echoed when he played cards and drank bourbon with my daddy.

"Do you remember Lincoln Storey from the old days?" I asked, remembering my father's words about him from so long ago.

"Nope, I try not to remember too much about the old days."

"He grew up in your and daddy's neighborhood. Daddy told me once Storey's father used to beat him up when he was a kid.

Funny the things you remember. I remember daddy saying it like it was yesterday."

"Your daddy was something else, Puddin'. I loved him like a brother." Jackson pulled out a cigarette and dragged on it, savoring it. The kettle began to whistle and he got up, poured some boiling water into a china cup, dropped a lemon mist tea bag into it, and brought it back over to the table.

"So what brings you out here to see this old man today?"

"Did you know they arrested Tasha Green for killing him?" I asked as I took a sip of tea.

"That's what they been saying," he said, his eyes darkening suddenly, sadness I assumed. I thought about DeLorca. He'd called it right when he'd said how fast word was traveling on this one. I also noticed that the bottle of merlot that Jackson had brought to the table was half empty. Had he and Brandon Pike shared some wine?

"I'm working for Tasha Green's sister," I said. "She wants me to find out who really killed Storey."

"You don't think she did it?" he asked evenly, his eyes searching mine.

I sighed. "I don't know, Jackson. It might have been an accident. I don't think she meant to do it, if she did, but she had a motive, that was for sure. He pulled some pretty raunchy stuff on her, and she was pretty young when he started sleeping with her. You knew they were sleeping together?''

"That was one of Storey's many problems. He couldn't keep his hands off the help."

"They say they have two witnesses that heard her say something about killing him with peanuts that night he had that first attack. Do you remember?''

He nodded as if he were tired.

"Tasha thinks that one of them was somebody named Minnie. Was he sleeping with her, too?'' *Minnie the hoochie.* Tasha's words describing the girl echoed in my mind.

"Minnie? Hell, no, he wasn't sleeping with Minnie. I hired Minnie. She's kin to me. Almost kin, anyway." He stumbled over that piece of information, but there was something about the way he said it that told me it was private information. "Minnie's married now to a good man. Has a little boy, almost three. Storey knew better than to look at Minnie out the side of his eye. Tasha said he was going with Minnie? Tasha was making that mess up!''

"Do you know who the person was who said Tasha had threatened Storey's life?'' I asked again.

"I think it was Minnie. I told her not to say nothing, but that girl is honest as a nun. If she knows the truth, she's going to tell it. I wasn't going to say nothing, though.''

Was somebody lying about Minnie and her relationship with Storey?

"Tasha said you were depressed about something that night? The night you were all here when he had that first reaction?"

He took a sip of wine and studied my face closely. "So that's what Tasha said?" There was an edge in his voice, a defensiveness with an undercurrent of anger. "Miss Tasha is full of tales, ain't she?" He snorted a laugh. "Naw, nothing was bothering me that night. I was mad at Lincoln. Half the time I saw him I was mad at him, but there wasn't nothing special about that night."

"Who does your place belong to now?" I asked, changing direction.

"Mrs. Storey, I guess. Want some more tea?" The phone rang in the office across the hall from the kitchen.

"Excuse me, Puddin'," Tate said and went into the office, closing the door behind him. When he came back he picked up my cup, placed another tea bag in it and some more hot water, and sat back down across from me. "That was Minnie, just now," he said, answering a question that I wouldn't have asked. "Miss Tasha had a big fight with him that night, too, the night he ate that sauce. Did she tell you that? Did she tell you she was pregnant with Storey's baby?" he said, throwing it out fast, like a nasty kid with a score to settle.

"How did you know that?" I asked quickly.

"I heard them arguing in the kitchen."

"That time a month ago, before he had the reaction?"

"Yeah. That's why she was here, to tell him. I guess he was through with her by then. Tasha grabbed him into the kitchen on the way back from the men's room. Wanted to know why he wasn't returning her calls. She was right nasty to him, and he was right nasty back."

"And who was there, in the kitchen when they had the fight?"

"Well, nobody was in the kitchen except me when they were arguing. But later on, when he got that peanut sauce, me, Tasha, Minnie, the Storeys, Brandon, Stella Pharr, lot of the same folks who were here on Friday were in the restaurant and in and out of the kitchen."

"What happened, Friday, just here in the kitchen? You were in and out pretty much from the beginning to the end of the night. Can you give me some sense of who else came and left? A sequence of events," I asked as I took out the black and white notebook that I always carry with me. Jackson looked at it doubtfully.

"Sequence of events? I don't know nothing about no sequence of events. What you going to do with that?" He nodded toward the notebook.

113

"Nothing, Jackson. I just want to get the times straight, that's all."

"I don't want nothing I say played back to no cops. Do you hear me?" He said it like I was six and he was telling me not to run across the street.

"I won't, Jackson. I just want to get a sense of what happened when."

"Okay. For your daddy's sake I'm going to tell you." He gave me a wink as if to let me know he wasn't really mad. "I had been here the night before, Thursday night, testing this new recipe I got for Ground Nut Stew, which was why all that peanut butter was sitting out there on the counter. The storage space was filled with stuff for the party so there wasn't no room for it in there, and the Deltas had asked me to cater a party for them with some West African food about a month from now. I wanted to be ready for that. If I'd known somebody was going to kill the man with that peanut butter, I'd—" The sentence dropped off, and he looked at me and shook his head, and began again. "I was here late Thursday night, so I came in around four on Friday. Tasha came to set things up around six."

"She brought the bean dip with her?"

"Yeah. She brought everything with her. Mr. Storey came in around seven. We had a few words, me and Mr. Storey, and then he started arguing with me about hiring Tasha to do the catering. I didn't know that things

114

were that bad between them. Then him and Tasha got into it. Something about her getting thrown out of her house, and then they started arguing about the baby, and he called the girl a ho' and she slapped him across the mouth, and he slapped her back, hard as a motherfucker, excuse my language, Puddin'. There wasn't nothing I could do but stand there like a fool and look, but I could tell she was mad as the dickens. I felt bad for the girl, though. I really did."

"The party officially started at around eight?" I asked.

"People started to come in good around eight-thirty. Stella Pharr came in around eight. You saw them talking in the kitchen here, around what time? Eight-fifty or so? Before Tasha came in here cursing with her filthy mouth. After that I went on with my serving, helped Tasha fix a few things in here 'cause I could see she was upset. And that was about it."

He lit another cigarette and took a long swallow of his wine, finishing what was left in his glass.

"Does that help you out?"

"Thanks, Jackson," I said knowing that was all I would get. "Do you know if Tasha was going with anybody else?"

"I never seen nobody else around here."

"What about the rest of the family? Anything strange about them—Alexa? Mrs. Storey? Brandon?''

Tate visibly flinched, and then nodded his head.

"Nope."

"Jackson, how did he get a piece of your restaurant?" I asked as I was putting my notebook back into my pocketbook, a toss-away question but the one that had haunted me from the first day Storey walked into my office and told me.

Tate picked up his glass and my cup, got up and rinsed them out in the sink, and placed them on the drainboard.

"Your daddy always told me I was a greedy son of a bitch. That's what your daddy always called me. But he said it with a laugh not to hurt me none, just to let me know. Lincoln Storey knew that about me the same as if I'd told him that myself. Greed, Puddin'. The same way a con man knows a mark will go for his game, that's what Lincoln knew about me, that was all."

"And that's all there was? Your greed?"

"Yeah," he said simply, his eyes leaving mine for an instant and then returning. There had to be more to it, but that stubbornness in Tate's eyes, the hard set of his jaw, told me I wasn't going to hear it tonight, so I let it lay.

"So when you going to bring that boy by to see me?" He added it in quickly, smiling now.

"I was thinking of doing it on his birthday.

116

Whenever I can get together the . . ." I stopped, realizing that Tate probably didn't want to hear my money woes any more than I wanted to tell them. "Whenever I can get some time," I finished unconvincingly.

"Whenever you want to bring that boy in here, come on and everything is on me. I'll never be that broke where I can't feed my best friend's grandbaby." He gave my hand a squeeze.

We stood up, and I gave him a hug then, feeling the rough texture of his sweater against my cheek, the sour smell of tobacco and alcohol reminding me so much of my father, it made my eyes water.

"It's been good talking to you, Jackson." I meant it from the bottom of my heart.

"Yeah, it has," he answered, but distractedly, as if something was weighing heavily on his mind. "Puddin', you done your daddy proud. You done him proud the same way he done you."

I left Tate's place feeling good, warmed by his benediction. I had verified some of what Tasha had told me about the people who'd been there during the first reaction—the same folks who had been there for his last.

It was dark by the time I got out of Belvington Heights. I turned toward the Parkway, and then decided to take the other route, which was scenic by day but longer by night. But it would end up closer to the Pathmark near my house, and I realized I'd better stop and pick up some coffee. I was getting as tired as hell of tea.

Tomorrow. I'll worry about this mess tomorrow, I thought to myself, and I realized, as my stomach started growling, that I hadn't eaten since breakfast.

Jamal and I have a running agreement that he is supposed to start dinner when I run late, but his menus usually consist of baked chicken wings and drumsticks with barbecue sauce poured over them with Green Giant canned creamed corn for vegetables on the side. I hoped I had a can of tuna fish or Goya black bean soup stored away somewhere in the pantry.

I riffled through the tapes in the glove compartment, trying to find a Cassandra Wilson, found Toni Braxton instead, and popped it into the cassette player and began singing along as I shifted the Blue Demon into fourth trying to remember if I had enough white musk bubble bath left for a hot bath.

The road was curvier and darker than I remembered it. I snapped on my high beams to shed some light on the situation. My headlights flickered and danced off the foliage lining the sides of the road. I glanced back in my rearview mirror, out of habit more than anything else. Nothing but blackness lay behind or before me. The houses—starting at about half a million apiece—were all set back from the road, shielded from public view by thick shrubbery.

Even though it was early, I realized I hadn't seen another car since I'd turned onto the road from Tate's. The huge oaks and pines that shadowed the road made the way seem darker, lonelier. I stepped on the gas, anxious to make some time.

It was then I noticed the car coming up over a hill behind me: Two creeping beams of light were on my tail. I breathed a sigh of relief. It was good to have company. At least I wasn't the only one out here. Except for the roar and occasional cough of my car, it was as quiet as if I'd dropped off the edge of the earth. I turned up Toni until the car rocked with rhythm.

If Jamal could see me now, I'd never get him to turn his stereo down.

I glanced back at the headlights. They were still there, closer than before. I could see the car now clearly, despite the darkness.

It was a black Honda Accord trimmed in gold with tinted windows, no license plate in the front. I couldn't make out whoever was driving; the beams were too bright.

It started with a tap, lightly hitting the back of my car. I drove faster, alarmed, wondering if I should pull off to the side of the road. Whoever it was knew this curvy piece of the road better than I did; I ought to let whoever it was lead the way. I wasn't getting it.

But then it happened again. Harder this time, ramming my car so hard I lost my breath, knocking my hands off the wheel, my chest hurled into the steering wheel.

"Shit!" I screamed out loud. "Damn it!"

It rammed me again, and I drove faster as panic hit me. I began to sweat, under my arms, between my thighs; the muscles in the bottom of my stomach began to twitch.

They were trying to hurt me.

Could it be kids bent on taking my car? I'd heard that was the way they carjacked sometimes, bumping somebody like they'd hit her, forcing her off the road, then pulling a gun. But the absurdity of that notion struck me the moment it crossed my mind. Who would want the Blue Demon?

It was me they were after.

And somehow, I knew it was "they."

One to watch. One to follow. One to drive. One to shoot?

I pushed the gas peddle down then. The car shook and the engine raced, but I pushed it further, down to the floor, taking curves at fifty, sixty miles an hour, praying for the sound of a siren behind me. But there was nothing, just blackness and silence and the other car now, keeping right up with me.

I pushed the car into fifth gear, which I hadn't used in so long I'd forgotten that I had it. Up one hill down the next, but the Honda was behind me, snapping at my heels like a dog from hell.

I made a sharp turn fast to the right, driving over the curve of the road through some shrubbery into somebody's driveway, stopping short before I hit a white stone fence, and in the next moment I switched off my lights. My heart was beating so hard I could feel it in my throat.

What did they want from me?

I locked the doors on all sides, then slumped back against the seat, staring out through the mirror, waiting in terror. Headlights as bright as cat's eyes came behind me, slowed, then went on their way. I took a deep breath, shaking like a kid. I looked around now, finally getting my bearings.

I could see somebody's mansion, stately and big, looming just up ahead. I was probably on the outskirts of Belvington Heights. Several cars were passing now, on their way: home from work, to the grocery store. Normal street sounds—a horn from somewhere, a dog barking, the screech of tires—surrounded me again. I said a prayer, then sat for a moment to catch my breath. Then I shifted the Blue Demon into first and started home.

But I couldn't shake the thought that made my hair stand up on the back of my neck: Whoever had hit my car knew where I'd been. And they probably knew where I was going.

9

"**S**o what kind of tea is that?" Jamal asked me. I'd just splashed a shot of Courvoisier into a china teacup and was bolting it down as he walked into the kitchen.

"It's not tea."

"How come you're drinking in the middle of the day?"

"It's not the middle of the day."

"Middle of the week."

"I'm an adult," I said, sounding like a kid. "And I'm old enough to have an occasional glass of wine after work if I feel like it."

"A glass of *wine*, Ma?" He opened the oven, took out a pan of glazed, slightly burned chicken and glanced at me over his shoulder. "Are you okay?"

"Fine." I rinsed out the teacup, screwed the top back on the cognac, and put it back on the shelf where it belonged, keeping my hands busy so he couldn't see them shaking.

"You sure?"

"Have I ever lied to you?"

He rolled his eyes, and we both started laughing. Only then did I realize suddenly how much I needed to laugh. Jamal must have wondered why I was laughing so hard at something that wasn't that funny.

"But you always tell me the truth when it's something big time, right?" he asked when we'd stopped laughing, the concern still there.

"Yeah. I always tell you the truth, son—" I paused—"sooner or later."

He rolled his eyes, heaped some chicken wings swimming in barbecue sauce and buttered creamed corn on a plate, handed it to me, and got another one for himself. I wolfed the food down like a kid with a cholesterol jones, so distracted I forgot to thank him for fixing my plate for me.

"Well, I see you're finally starting to appreciate my cooking," he said with a grin. I glanced up, my mind somewhere else and nodded.

We ate in silence. I thumbed through the *Star-Ledger* without really reading it while Jamal studied a history textbook. When we'd finished, he gathered up his book, a notebook, and a couple of oatmeal raisin cookies from an Archway bag, and headed back to his room. I started scraping the dishes humming "I Apologize" from an Anita Baker CD like I didn't have a care in the world. But I was scared shitless.

The car seemed to have come from nowhere, but it must have been behind me, just out of sight all the way from Tate's. Only two people, as far as I knew, were aware that I'd been there: Jackson Tate, whom I'd known all my life, who had carried my father's coffin at his funeral, and Brandon Pike, whose fine lean body I'd once known as intimately as my own.

When I finished the dishes, I said good night to Jamal and found that white musk bubble bath and settled into a hot tub filled to the brim with fragrant bubbles. Before I went to bed, I put the double locks on the doors and windows, and I got out of bed and checked them again before I went to sleep for good.

I woke up the next morning at 10:45, mad because I'd slept so late. Jamal had slapped a Post-it on the refrigerator telling me he had basketball practice and would be home late. I went into the kitchen in search of coffee, got mad again when I realized I hadn't had a chance to buy it, and hurled a mild curse at the kettle as I filled it with water, banged it on the stove, and tossed two Lipton teabags into a cup.

I had dreamed about my mother, but I could only remember the edges of it and the loud angry sound of her voice screaming at me to do something. I had not been able to cry when she died. Maybe I never will cry for her, and that frightens me more than anything else about my life. I was angry at everybody for a while: at my father for his drinking hard, at my aunt for trying to raise me and then giving up to let me raise myself.

I lived my twenties—through my first marriage and Jamal's early years—fast and in a daze, reeling from all that pain. I'm not sure when I recovered, if I have, but I just realized at some point that Jamal was all that was left from any of them, and there was no sense in dwelling in the past. I had to take care of business or it would take care of me.

I finished the tea and a bowl of Cheerios, slipped into a skirt, blouse, heels and stockings—sometimes just dressing like a professional will get you in the mood to work—and headed out.

It was sunny, and the tulips the guy next door had planted were putting my yard to shame. Squirrels think my yard is their personal pleasure resort; everything I plant they uproot. I also forget to water my little patch, so needless to say, I don't have many flowers save the dandelions, my most dependable plant.

Last night's fear seemed almost funny today now that the sun was shining bright. I glanced up and down the street good, searching for anything or anybody who looked like they didn't belong, but nothing was there except what should have been: one-family houses, lawns that would soon need mowing, a bike or two left in a driveway by some careless kid.

I checked the back of my car and then opened the trunk and checked the contents. The usual junk and the tools of my trade that I don't keep in my house or office were still there: an extra flashlight with a couple of packs of batteries, two or three different size screwdrivers, a jackknife, two extra rolls of film for my Polaroid, two wigs—one long pageboy, one short Afro wig—courtesy of Wyvetta, three pairs of cheap sunglasses that I'd picked up at Penn station, a floppy straw hat that made me look like I'd just finished picking a row of cotton, and a cigar box, a gift from Randy, this sweet little hoodlum I used to go with in high school, which was filled with lock-picking tools he'd inherited from his uncle: a "nose-puller" for rapid lock removal, a couple of blank keys cut in different sizes, an awl, a shimming tool, and a cordless drill with an 1/8 inch twist bit.

I kept my eyes glued on the backview mirror on the way to my office, even though it was high noon, and when I got to my building I glanced up and down the street before I got out of my car. Nothing.

I peeked into the Biscuit as I walked into the building Wyvetta and I shared. The two women who work for Wyvetta—the one who does the weaves and the other who does nails and tips—were chatting excitedly. There was no sign of Wyvetta yet; I figured she'd canceled all her appointments. I stopped at the mailbox to get my mail, and waved at the women without stopping. I'd bet money they were talking about Tasha and Storey. On a good day in the Biscuit, you could find out anything you wanted to know about anybody in Essex County by the time you got your perm and tips done. Those two sisters loved to talk some trash—and Lincoln Storey and Tasha Green were some serious trash.

The shadow of the orphan aloe, the aloe plant abandoned at my door about a year ago by somebody who never owned up to it, looked sinister against the drawn shades in my office. I snapped on the lights and pulled the shades up; dusty sunlight filtered in, shedding light on my secondhand computer, two matching chairs, and the small table in the corner topped by my electric kettle, the three opened boxes of Celestial Seasonings tea, and the small black and white TV that I watch the soaps on when things are slow, which is most of the time.

"How you doing? Need some water?" I asked the orphan aloe as I closed the door behind me. I talk to my plant sometimes; half the time I almost expect it to answer. I hung my coat up, dropped my unopened mail on a corner of the desk, and turned on my computer. I filled my electric kettle with water from the bathroom down the hall as I waited for it to boot up. I poured some water on the orphan aloe, plugged in the kettle, then plopped down in front of my computer wondering when I'd be able to stash away enough cash to buy a kettle that didn't take fifteen minutes to reach a boil.

A chill went through me as I sat down in my chair and remembered the last time I'd sat here, flashing my teeth and facing Lincoln Storey, who'd been seated in one of the empty chairs that faced me now.

I owed him.

That thought came from nowhere with the clarity of some ancient truth, which I couldn't shake.

I owed him.

For the thousand bucks he'd paid me in good faith. And on GP. Because DeLorca was right. Once a cop, always a cop, and somebody had offed the man right in my face, and I had no idea who had done it or why, and that bugged the hell out of me.

When the kettle finally whistled, I dropped a red zinger tea bag into my company cup and poured boiling water over it. Then I settled back into my chair, typing DBBD—Death By Bean Dip—into the space to name the file, and waited for some inspiration.

When it didn't come, I walked to the window and dabbed away the excess water that had pooled on the window sill under the orphan aloe with a Kleenex, then sat back down and stared at the computer again.

Starting with A, I typed the names of all the people who Tasha and Jackson said had seen Storey's first allergic reaction: *Alexa Storey, Brandon Pike, Daphne Storey, Minnie the hoochie* (despite Tate's defense of the girl, she remained "the hoochie"), *Jackson Tate, Stella Pharr, Tasha Green.*

Seven people. Seven suspects? Six if I gave my girl Tasha a break and deleted her name, which just for the hell of it I did, then typed it back in at the end of the list. It hurt to put Jackson's name up there, but fair was fair, despite old times.

Which of them would want Storey dead? With the exception of Stella Pharr, nearly everyone up there was better off with Storey gone.

Alexa Storey. Both she and her mother would benefit from Storey's death. And she'd have Brandon, too, no strings attached. Those were two serious motives.

Brandon Pike. With Storey out of the way he could continue to go with Alexa with Storey's money that she could inherit. Acquiring money was Brandon's dearest goal. He was high on my list, right up there with his girlfriend.

And then there was Daphne of the king-size rock and flawless skin. She certainly had a motive, the oldest there was. Follow the money and you'll find the one who kills for it. *Unless there's more than one who will kill for it.* But Tasha said he had found the "love of his life again."

Minnie. Tate's "almost kin." I only had Jackson's word against Tasha's on that one, and it was my own prejudice that made me assume that it was Tate who was telling the truth. And what about Minnie with those fake eyes and fake hair. Could have been Storey's type, for all I knew.

Jackson Tate. If Storey were dead, he might get his restaurant back; and what he had on Jackson, if he did have something, would die with him. Jackson wasn't telling me everything. *What was he holding back?* And what if Minnie had been involved with Storey? What if Tate hadn't liked it because he knew what a son of a bitch Lincoln was? Lincoln had Tate by his balls, and he'd seen how he treated Tasha, "slapping her across the mouth" even though he knew she was pregnant. Could protecting Minnie be a motive for murder? Protecting Minnie and hating Storey's guts? Honor. I had seen men kill for less. And what was to become of Tate's place now that Storey was dead?

Stella Pharr? All I knew about her was that she looked like she needed some fast fun in the sun and a good laxative. I typed a question mark next to her name and wrote Jake's name in big letters next to it. What was her real involvement with Lincoln? I thought I'd seen real intimacy between them when I'd stumbled upon them sitting in the kitchen, but what role could she have played in Storey's death?

And that brought me to the end of the list, back to Miss Tasha with the B-girl attitude.

When I lined up the mess on Tasha, the list looked like the one the D.A. was probably working from. *Motive:* Money *and* revenge. You couldn't beat those. Storey had treated her like yesterday's lunch, slapping her around in front of Jackson, causing her to be humiliated in front of her neighbors. And if he were the father of her baby-to-be and she could prove it, she'd probably be entitled to a generous settlement from the estate, particularly if his stepdaughter was willing to verify their relationship. Daphne Storey might be willing to pay some big bucks just to protect her dead husband's good name. But mainly there was revenge. *Opportunity:* Ole Tasha had plenty of that. *Means:* Tasha had, as De-Lorca put it, done the bean dip that done him in. Storey had told me that "he liked a woman with spirit," and he'd certainly gotten some spirit with my girl.

But did she have enough spirit to kill him?

And there was that "little something" on the side. I'd known many a "little something" who could change the rules of the game before you even knew he was playing. I saved the screen and splashed some more hot water on my teabag, no additional insight coming.

I looked at my watch; it wasn't quite 2:30. Too early to go home and call it a good day's work, too late to go out for lunch. I picked up the mail that I'd tossed on the table earlier and started sorting through it, hurling the junk mail into the trash, tearing open the bills, glancing at them, shaking my head in disgust, and putting them in a separate pile.

I opened my life-insurance bill, first noting with satisfaction that it wasn't due for another two weeks. I could handle that. But seeing it made me remember that I still hadn't paid another one—my health-insurance bill, which was due in two days. I'd circled the date with a red Magic Marker and left it standing on my bureau so I wouldn't forget it, which, of course, I had.

I muttered a curse, wondering if Storey's check had cleared yet. With any luck it had, and I could drop the check in the mail on the way home. I looked on the back of my ATM card for the 800 number and quickly dialed it. My balance, pitifully low, told me that the money from Storey hadn't come in. The computer voice invited me to press O to talk to a live, twenty-four-hour operator which I did to find out just how much longer the check would take.

A high nasal voice finally came on the line, which I envisioned belonging to a thin, peevish woman with a large nose. I asked her about Storey's check, trying to keep from sounding as anxious as I was.

"A stop payment was placed on that check this morning," she said matter-of-factly.

"Stop payment!" I screamed into the phone, knocking over the cup of red zinger onto my desk, then mopping it up fast with my sleeve before it got to my computer. "What do you mean?"

Silence on the other end.

"Stop payment!" I screamed again.

"Miss—" she began. "I can only—"

"What do you mean the payment has been stopped?" I knew I was carrying on like a fool, but I couldn't help it. "Why?" I cried as if she'd know.

"Miss, I suggest you check with your bank tomorrow," she said like she was talking to a difficult child. The line went dead then and I was left glaring at the chair across from me as if Storey's butt were still warming it.

What do you do when a rich man with a nasty attitude gives you a thousand-dollar retainer and then drops dead? If you're broke like me with a son who likes sports and a health insurance bill due in two days, you consider it a gift from the universe.

What do you do when the payment is stopped? Go a little crazy, which is what I did

133

as I sat in that chair, tears streaming down my face like a kid.

Maybe I hadn't earned the whole thousand dollars, but I had earned a percentage of it. Even fifty dollars would bring me closer to paying the bills I had to pay every month. I'd gone to Tate's, as Storey requested. Checked out the scene, as he'd requested. Begun a surveillance of Brandon Pike, in a fashion. And what was fifty dollars to the estate of Lincoln Storey? To Daphne Storey? And anyway, was that all the grieving widow had on her mind, stopping payment on my check?

I got mad then—mad at Lincoln Storey, at Daphne Storey, and then finally at myself for how much I'd really been counting on that money, how I seemed always up against the wall with every bill I owed.

The phone rang, and I let it ring twice, then grabbed it before Karen, the girl who answers my calls for my answering service, did—if she would; I hadn't paid that bill yet either.

"Hello," I said dully, my voice reflecting how I felt.

"Tamara?" the voice on the other end asked. "You okay? You sound down."

It was probably the only person in the world who could have brought me out of it.

I have known Jake since we were kids when I spotted him that first time playing basketball with Johnny in our backyard. He was younger than Johnny and was one of the young guys on the block who looked up to and loved my brother as if he belonged to them. He's still as good-looking as he was then, but there's gray mixed in now with that beautiful dark hair, and a sad, hard-won wisdom in his eyes. He's also fine, to put it bluntly, and one of the fondest memories of my young adolescence is watching him, shirtless in a pair of tight red gym shorts, sweat glistening on his muscular arms and legs, standing poised to shoot a basketball on a hot summer day. He had definitely played an active role in my early sexual fantasies.

He is always there for anybody in the neighborhood who needs him: He serves as a Scout master even though he doesn't have a son; as a delivery boy for the old lady who lives down the block. And he's what my father used to call a "race man": One of those brothers who will always fight the good fight, a living challenge to every lie that was ever told about black folks—a man in the tradition of Malcolm X, Frederick Douglass, Nelson Mandela—but with the kind of body hot dreams are made of.

I have spent the last decade of my life falling in and out of love with this man, not admitting it to anybody, including myself half the time. He has spent the last decade of his coming to my rescue—half friend, half big brother—whenever I needed him.

His wife, Phyllis, the first love of his life,

has become the most painful part these days. She is what the old folks would call crazy, but I'm sure there's some clinical name for her problem. She spends time in and out of institutions. Jake is too good a man to leave her.

Jake has a sixth sense that makes him one of the best defense attorneys in the business. Somehow this sense always seems to make him call me when he's the only person in the world I want to talk to. Like today.

"So things are okay?"

"The usual," I said glumly.

"Money?"

"The damn health-insurance bill came in."

"You know, Tam, I owe you that money for taking Denise to get that ballet stuff last month when Phyllis was—"

"Don't even mention that, Jake. That little bit of money I spent—"

"Let me give it to you now, while I have it."

"Jake, I get tired of borrowing money—"

"You know what you and Jamal mean to me. What Johnny meant."

We were both silent then. The feelings we share aren't easily defined or explained—they never have been—but Johnny is a part of them, and Phyllis is, too. I can't deny that.

"Listen, I was calling to find out if you and Jamal like oysters?"

"Oysters? Yeah, sure. I love them."

"They had a big sale at Pathmark. I got

about four pints of them. Got them home, looked at them good, and noticed the date that you can't use them after is the day after tomorrow. There's no way in hell I can eat all these oysters in two days. Phyllis won't eat them, she says they give her gas, and Denise is on some diet, some fruit thing."

We both laughed. His daughter, a few years younger than Jamal and just entering adolescence, was suddenly consumed with clothes, makeup, and the body perfect.

"Sure, drop them off. Jake, there's something else I want to talk to you about, anyway," I said.

"Want to go into it now?"

"No," I said. "Later on when you come by."

I wanted to know if he had anything on Lincoln Storey. And if he could shed some light on Stella Pharr. Jake is the only person I ever talk to about my cases. I trust his instincts, his sense of people, and the bad things they are capable of. And that made me think about the mess with the car. The fear came back, but I shook it away.

"Tonight?" I asked. My voice was louder than I'd intended.

"Yeah, see you later." If Jake had detected my anxiety, he didn't say.

After he'd hung up, I walked over to the window again, plucked a leaf off the aloe, watched the gel ooze up, all the time watching the cars go by, not telling myself I was thinking about the way that Honda had knocked the breath out of me. The car wasn't there, just the usual folks walking up and down Main Street.

I sat back down, thinking about the money again, and what I could have done with that thousand that didn't clear.

Should I call the woman? I pulled Storey's card out of my wallet where I'd jammed it on Friday and checked the address: 9 Hillside Drive, Belvington Heights. No telephone number except the one he'd jotted down. I sat back down and glanced again at my computer, and that first name popped from the list, like it was asking for my attention. *Alexa Storey.*

Alexa Storey. Daphne Storey.

The daughter and mother who had brought back the memory of my mother so strongly I'd dreamed about her last night.

Alexa Storey.

What had those frightened, restless eyes been hiding Friday night?

Maybe it was time I found out.

10

Some folks just didn't want to believe that a black man could live as grand as Lincoln Storey did, and when he bought the old Mincer Place, a turn-of-the-century mansion perched on the highest hill in Belvington Heights, there were those who thought he shouldn't live there.

A nigger don't deserve to live as good as that.

I'd heard talk like that when I'd been in the Department, usually from those who worked in the town but couldn't afford to live in it.

But other folks reveled in Lincoln Storey's success, grinned about it, bragged about it to their kids.

Work and save your money and you can eat as high on the hog as Lincoln Storey does.

I didn't know how high on Mr. Hog Lincoln Storey had dined, but he was rich enough never to have to worry about his car needing a new transmission or paying a health-insurance bill.

There were no numbers marking the driveways tucked out of sight on Hillside Drive—people who didn't know where they were going had no business being here. As I drove down the road looking for Storey's place, I wished for luck when I turned into the fifth tree-shaded driveway. The old Mincer Place, the Storey place now (which I recognized because it had been featured in *Ebony* about a year ago), loomed large on the right as soon as I turned the first bend.

The Storey mansion was four stories of brown and gray brick topped by a weathered slate roof and graced with groupings of ceiling-to-floor circletop windows that sparkled in the sunlight. The neat, well-pruned foliage and flowers that blossomed in the front yard hinted at a gardener's TLC; those squirrels who carried on their mess at my place wouldn't dare flash their furry little butts around here. The lawn that extended to the sides and toward the hills in the distance looked as green and smooth as astro turf, and the massive shade trees that swayed in the breeze looked older than the Emancipation Proclamation.

I sat in my car for a moment, awestruck by the serene beauty of the place. Despite everything I knew about the man, I was suddenly proud of Lincoln Storey, whose young behind old Seafus Storey had beat up and down Belmont Avenue. Whatever else Storey had done—and he had done some mess—he'd made himself into something, as Wyvetta would say. He had climbed hard, long, and fast. I had to give the brother that.

I walked toward the house. Birds chirped noisily and a wind chime tinkled somewhere in the distance. I rang the doorbell, half expecting a doorman with tails and an attitude to open the door. I was almost as surprised to see Alexa Storey, dressed in jeans and a long-sleeved knit shirt, as she was to see me. She'd obviously been expecting somebody else, and the smile on her face dropped. I wondered why she hadn't bothered to look through the peephole.

She looked stronger today, prettier, more confident than she'd looked Friday night. Her skin, scrubbed clean of makeup, glowed as fresh as a kid's, and the acne scars were less noticeable. The long-sleeved red-and-blue striped shirt with a Polo emblem at the neckband flattered her, and her dark brown hair hung loosely down her back.

"Good afternoon, I'm Tamara Hayle, a private investigator. I'm working for Wyvetta Green. Tasha Green's sister." I used my pert, professional voice, getting right to the point as quickly as I could. "If you have a minute or two, I was hoping you would be kind enough to answer a few questions. If this isn't a good time—"

"Tasha?" she asked, interrupting me, as if that was the only word she'd heard from my spiel.

"Tasha Green," I repeated, sensing my in. "She mentioned that you two were close friends." Tasha hadn't said anything about close, but I figured I'd toss it in for the hell of it.

"How is she? Is she okay?" Alexa asked anxiously, the questions falling out one on top of the other.

"You heard then, that she was arrested Monday morning for your stepfather's murder."

"I heard." Alexa cast her eyes down, as if just remembering Storey's demise. Not a lot of grieving here. "She didn't do it, though," she added quickly, her confidence in Tasha's innocence outstripping mine.

"I agree with you," I said, in what I hoped was a convincing voice. "You won't mind then if I ask you and your mother a few questions. We, Ms. Green and I, don't think Tasha is guilty, either, and we want to get to the bottom of this before it goes any further." I hoped using the "we" would add some authority to my plea.

"Bottom of this?"

"What really happened. If it's a bad time—"

I asked again. Alexa looked puzzled for a minute, like she didn't quite understand me.

"Is it okay if I come in?"

Without saying anything she stepped aside, tacitly giving me permission to enter. I stepped into the foyer before she could change her mind.

A graceful curved staircase divided the house into two halves, and sets of double French doors on either side concealed, I imagined, various rooms: a library, dining room, living room, study.

"My mother's in the den," Alexa said, leading the way across parquet floors as shiny and smooth as marble.

"How many bedrooms do you have?" I asked, gawking like a tourist, regretting the words the minute they were out of my mouth.

"Eight, nine if you count the upstairs study as one, which we don't," she answered nonchalantly as we walked. "We're looking for an additional housekeeper if you know of anybody. We have someone part-time, but we need somebody here everyday. Do you know anybody who does daywork?"

"Daywork? Me? No." I snapped too quickly. *I knew somebody, but she's dead.* "Good help is hard to find, huh?" I said It with a bitchy twist that I regretted the moment it was out. Alexa looked surprised and then shrugged like she'd caught that kind of attitude from people all her life.

"It doesn't matter one way or the other to me," she said defensively. "I'd live in a studio apartment and wash my own dishes if I could. It's my mother. She is one of those women who has always had others do for her, never had to dirty her hands with anything she didn't want to touch. Sometimes I think she was created to fill other people's fantasies and that's what she's finally become—the sum total of her lesser parts and other people's dreams." She said it with a little laugh that was probably meant to cut the bitterness, but it was wasted on me.

"Honey, you sure are hard on Moms." I was startled by her honesty.

"Let's put it this way," Alexa said quietly. "The only time our mother-daughter thing plays good is on holidays." Her words and the way she said them went straight to where they lived within me.

"Could I ask you something, Alexa?" I asked, slowing down a bit, wanting to get some questions in before we reached her mother. Her friendship with Tasha had puzzled me the minute I'd heard about it, and I was curious to know how they'd met. From the way Alexa and Daphne had gone at each other in the ladies' room on Friday and from what she'd just said, I knew they didn't share mother-daughter confidences, and I'd bet that Tasha—with her big mouth and bigger attitude—was not one of those friends Alexa

144

brought home to Mommy, particularly since Tasha was doing Daddy on the side. If I had any questions to ask Alexa about Tasha, now was the time to ask them.

"Depends on what your question is," Alexa answered my question, suspicious.

"How did you and Tasha get to be friends—if you don't mind my asking?"

"We used to hang at the same clubs. In New York, when we were younger."

"Your father—your stepfather—met her through you?"

"Yeah. I owe Tasha one for that."

"And you know about the baby."

Alexa stopped short. "So she's telling everybody now? That's her right, I guess. Yeah. I know about the baby. He had a way of putting his dick where it didn't belong."

I paused, startled by her words. "Did your stepfather ever act in an inappropriate way toward you?" *Putting his dick where it didn't belong, like maybe too near you, his young stepdaughter.* I wasn't sure where this angle would take me, but there was a glimmer of something that I couldn't read in Alexa's face.

"Inappropriate?"

"In ways that made you uncomfortable," I said, sounding like a social worker.

She turned away from me and started walking again.

"Everything about that man made me uncomfortable."

"How long had he and your mother been married?"

"Ever since my father died," she added with a bitter edge.

"The night your stepfather had that first attack, you were at Tate's for some kind of celebration, something to do with Ms. Pharr's campaign for the state assembly?"

"Yeah?" She turned to face me again, a shadow lingering in those restless eyes.

"You were one of the witnesses who told the cops about what Tasha had said about your stepfather that night, about the allergic reaction being a good way to take him out. It was you, wasn't it?" I was just fishing, bullying her almost. Alexa stopped short, grabbing my arm so tightly it hurt. I pulled away, shocked and surprised by the strength in those hands, and by the fear in her eyes.

"Someone told them that? It wasn't me, I swear it wasn't me. Please don't tell Tasha that I did that to her. She'd never forgive me, and I couldn't live with that."

"Who was it then?"

"I would never do that to Tasha."

"Who then?"

She looked like she wasn't going to say anything for a moment, and then she pursed her lips into a snide smile that was close to a sneer. "Maybe you should ask Mrs. Lincoln Storey," she said with a contemptuous nod

146

toward the family room. "Why don't you ask her?"

The room we entered, with its exposed beams crossing the ceiling and ferns and spider plants dangling against the windows, looked made to order for Daphne Storey. She was reclining on a leather couch, eating ice cream. A big screen TV in the corner was tuned in to *Oprah*. When we entered, she sat up, placed her ice cream down on the table in front of her, and snapped off *Oprah* with the remote as if she were coming to attention. She glanced from Alexa to me, then finally back to her daughter, a question in her eyes.

"This is Tamara Hayle," Alexa said, answering those eyes with a gesture toward me as she slid into one of a set of chairs across the coffee table from her mother. "She's a private investigator. She wants to find out what happened to your husband." She spat out the words "your husband," and I wondered how she could carry around so much bitterness for so long. The toughness in her voice and in the way she tilted her head brought back my eavesdropping session in the john, but she was the tough one now, the one in control.

Daphne's eyes lingered on her daughter and then switched to the TV set she'd just turned off and then finally came to rest on mine. She looked older than she had on Friday, but the beauty was still there, even though the roots of her dark hair peeked out from the bottom of her stylish cut. Her hands gave her away, though. There was a roughness around her pale knuckles that even the sparkle of the king-size rock couldn't hide.

The only thing a dark girl can do is lead me to a light one.

The words, teasing in a kid's dumb sing-song voice, popped into my mind suddenly from somewhere like some ugly obsessive thought.

You're too dark to be pretty; you must be smart.

I'd grown up during the 1960s, the Black Is Beautiful years, but that voice still fixed itself in the heads of kids like me, too loud to be silenced in a decade.

As Daphne Storey rose to meet me and extended her hand, I realized with unexpected shame that from the first moment I had seen her, I had judged her, disliked her because of the color of her skin, and for what I assumed that color had always brought her.

The pretty ones weren't supposed to look like me. They looked like Daphne Storey, with skin the color of cream and hair that cascaded down their backs: the only kind of black woman a "successful" black man like Lincoln Storey was supposed to want, the closest thing he could get to a white woman because he'd been told and believed that women who looked like his mother had no value.

If you're light, you're alright. If you're brown, stick around. If you're black, get back.

The color thing. I dropped my eyes, embarrassed to admit it to myself, but there it was. One black woman giving another grief for something that had nothing to do with either of them. I thought about Aunt Winnie then as I stood there holding Daphne's hand. Winnie, my father's favorite sister, my favorite aunt, so light most folks assumed she was white, but the strongest, toughest, blackest woman I'd ever known. The first to organize a march or protest when somebody pulled some mess, to take care of business when it needed taking care of.

The sting of color cut both ways. I remembered Winnie's bitterness when people made assumptions about her because of her light skin, and I was ashamed of myself for judging Daphne over foolishness like that, the way people used to judge my aunt.

What did I know of this woman's pain?

"How can I help you?" Daphne Storey asked, her voice soft with a girlish Southern lilt, bringing me back from my reverie. The voice was different from the one I'd heard arguing with her daughter.

Had I heard only what I wanted to hear?

"I know that you have suffered a terrible loss, Mrs. Storey, and I'm sorry to—"

She held up a hand to quiet me, then motioned for me to sit down next to her on the couch. The scent of Chanel filled my nose when I sat down beside her.

149

It had been my mother's favorite perfume, my father's last extravagant gift to her. She'd only worn it twice that I could remember. Her special scent for special occasions. The perfume that the women she worked for wore, she'd told me one day, warning me in the same breath never to touch it, which of course I had, the first moment I got, spilling out three capfuls and filling it up to the top with water for spite, and then being so ashamed of myself I couldn't sleep that night. I thought of my mother now as I sat next to Daphne, the smell of her perfume dulling my senses and bringing back my past and that shame.

"I'm sorry to barge in like this during your bereavement." I was suddenly aware of how unprepared I was to confront her. Lincoln Storey had become an abstraction to me, and Alexa's off-hand reaction to him had fed that notion. But I remembered Gilroy's observation of Daphne's cries of grief, her tears.

"I'm fine," she said to reassure me almost as if she were reading my mind. "Anything I can say or do to help you I'm glad to do it."

I saw Alexa shift in her seat and cross her arms, watching her mother closely.

"I'd like to extend my condolences to you and your family," realizing that I'd forgotten even to say that to Alexa as we'd stood on the porch.

"It was a shock. I don't think I've fully accepted it yet." She paused for a moment, and then continued, talking to me as if sharing a confidence, the way you do sometimes with people you hardly know.

"There were many things about my husband that I don't understand, that have come out since his death." She glanced at me then, with a slight, thin smile.

"Tasha Green?" I asked softly, wondering if I should bring her up but realizing that she must know about it anyway.

"There were many Tasha Greens."

"You know, then, that they are saying that she killed him."

"I've spoken to the police at least three times since his death. I don't know if Tasha Green is guilty. I don't know that it matters one way or the other." She sighed, her eyes studying something on the other side of the room. "He's dead now. I have the memories. Some good. Some so bad I don't even like to think about them. But I don't understand how I can help you with this. With Tasha Green and what she did."

"Then you think she's guilty?"

"She was angry at my husband, spreading lies about him. She hated him. Yes, I think she did it. I truly do."

"Is that why you told the police what you heard?"

"I didn't hear it, but when Jackson Tate, the owner of the restaurant, shared what he'd heard with me, I felt it was my responsibility to share it with the police, since Jackson wouldn't."

"That and the fact that you were mad about her sleeping with your husband."

She paused, her eyes suddenly full of pain. I wondered if I should have said that, if I had pushed things too far. But she smiled and then answered as if it didn't matter.

"Yeah, that too. And I hope that cheap, low-class little tramp rots in hell for what she did to Lincoln." The magnanimous tone of a few moments ago had vanished. Daphne picked up her bowl of ice cream and violently stirred the remains, which had melted.

"You really are a lying bitch, aren't you?" Alexa said evenly to her mother from across the room. We glanced up at her, both of us having forgotten her presence. "You should rot in hell for what you're trying to do to Tasha."

"Shut up. Just close your mouth!" Daphne's voice was soft but brutal.

That was all it took to defeat Alexa. With head down, she left the room, never so much as glancing in my direction, or in Daphne's.

"Do you have any children, Tamara?" with sudden chumminess.

"Yes, I have a son."

"Then you know how children can be. My daughter is angry about a lot of things. There's no way to tell who will be touched by that anger. No matter how old they are.

152

No matter how much you try to control them. My daughter is an embarrassment to me."

There was contempt in her voice when she said it and it made her voice hard, like the one I had overheard, like her daughter's when she'd spat out the word "bitch."

"I think you should know something about me, Mrs. Storey. I was working for your husband before he died. He had hired me to tail your daughter's boyfriend." The truth is all you've got sometimes, so I tossed it out. It seemed unfair, unethical not to tell her the whole truth. At first, she had no reaction.

"Oh, now I understand," she said softly. "I thought your name sounded familiar when Alexa mentioned it. Lincoln had written a check to you. One for a thousand dollars the day of his death?"

"Yes, your husband did write me a check for a thousand." I wondered why she bore no sense of surprise or outrage, why she hadn't asked why he had Brandon tailed, or when it started, or how long I'd been at it. I knew that Storey had hated Brandon. How did Daphne feel about him?

"You know, then, that I had the payment stopped on it."

"So I was told."

"I'm sorry. I had no idea what it was for. Our lawyers stopped payments on all large outgoing sums until we could review the accounts. Your check was particularly large so they asked me about it. If you'd like, you can rebill the estate; I'll make sure that that's taken care of. It won't be a problem now that I know what it was for."

"Thank you," I said, from the bottom of my heart. At least that question was answered.

"I thought you might be one of his women," she muttered almost as an afterthought.

"One of his women?"

"You know it's funny about me and Lincoln," she said almost playfully. "Most people wondered how I could stay with him, with the Tasha Greens and some of the others—no, I don't mind talking about it. It's over now.

"The truth was Lincoln and I loved each other. I guess you could say we'd rediscovered each other again in the last couple of months. I'm not sure what did it, how it happened, but our love for each other—and I know this may sound foolish, it probably would to many people—but our love had been renewed again. He had forgiven me for all my bitterness and I'd forgiven him for his infidelities. We had even talked about renewing our vows."

She sighed, and her eyes softened. "That's what is so ironic about the way things have turned out. For the first time in years, Lincoln and I seemed to be in love again." Tears filled her eyes and her voice cracked as she turned the big ring around and around on her finger. "It was as if we had rediscovered each other.

I won't say it was easy, but it was getting easier, and now it will be hard again. But he is dead, and I know I have to go on."

It's easy to tell if somebody is lying to you if you know what to look for. There's always a shifting of the eyes, an unwillingness to face you squarely. I once interviewed a woman who kept placing her fingers over her lips as if trying to prevent words from slipping out. Later when the real truth came out, I wasn't surprised to learn that she'd been lying through her teeth. But as Daphne's eyes, teary but steady, evenly returned my glance, I got the feeling she was giving me the real deal.

"How do you feel about Brandon Pike?" I asked her.

"I feel nothing one way or the other about Brandon Pike. He was my husband's problem," she said, her eyes not leaving mine. "I know that since this has happened, he has been a great help to our family. He has been there for me and my daughter like nobody else has."

The doorbell rang. "That's probably him now," she added. We both listened to Alexa's gasp of joy and the sound of a deep masculine voice answering her questions and teasing her good-naturedly as their footsteps tapped across the smooth-as-marble floors toward the room where we sat.

I knew I was the last person on Earth Brandon Pike expected to see sitting in the family room, but his face betrayed nothing but a slight twitch above the right eye, a controlled gesture of surprise that might have gone unnoticed by someone who didn't know him as well as I did.

"How are you doing, Mrs. Storey?" he asked formally, solicitously.

"I'm doing fine, Brandon, thank you." She tilted her face up toward him to kiss, which he did.

"Is there anything you want me to do? Any errand you want me to run?"

She nodded that there was nothing. "Do you know Ms. Tamara Hayle?"

"We've met," he said.

"More than once," I added, watching Brandon's shoulders straighten as he walked over to the bar and poured himself a drink.

"Can I get anybody anything?"

"I've got ice cream. Alexa?"

Alexa said nothing, she just stared straight ahead out the French doors toward the swimming pool.

"Is there anything else we can help you with?" Daphne asked me, suddenly impatient.

"No. I think that's about it."

"Can I walk you to your car then?" Brandon Pike asked abruptly, surprising everybody including me. Judging by the quick way he said it, I knew there was more to his offer than wanting to make sure I got to my car safely.

The two of us got up then, Brandon patting Alexa's head as you would a kid; I shook both women's hands in farewell.

"If you'd like to call my lawyer about that other matter, you should do it quickly," Daphne Storey said. "There will be no problem at all."

"Thank you," I said.

She picked the remote up and turned her attention back to the TV, raising the volume higher than it needed to be. Brandon closed the doors behind him. We didn't speak until we were clear of the house and near my car.

"This doesn't have anything to do with me, does it?" he asked me.

I looked up at him, surprised.

"What do you mean, anything to do with you?"

"With your being bitter about what went down between us. You coming by Tate's, then by here. Does it have anything to do with what we used to have?"

"Don't flatter yourself."

"What's going on, then?"

"I'm trying to find out who killed Lincoln Storey. I'm working for Tasha Green," I said simply.

"Then you must know she did it."

"I'm not so sure anymore."

"I'm warning you, Tamara, lay off Alexa

and Mrs. Storey," he said as if he were threatening me. "They didn't have anything to do with it. Mrs. Storey is grieving. Alexa's a kid. She can't take it. She's fragile. Why don't you just leave the whole thing alone, Tamara, before it's too late."

The level of my anger came so quickly it surprised even me. "You're warning me, Brandon? You're telling me to lay off? You, Mr. Kiss-anybody's-ass-for-a-dollar-and-a-half Pike? Have you forgotten that I *know* who you are?"

He flinched visibly as if I'd slapped him but recovered quickly. "Her father shot himself," he said bluntly. He took the key out of my hand and opened the door for me like a gentleman. "He shot himself through the mouth when she was a kid. A couple of months ago, Alexa tried to kill herself. She tried to do it when she was a kid, too. Those long sleeves she's always wearing. That dress on Friday and that thing she had on today covers the scars. The girl's at risk for suicide, Tamara. You know how that can be. You know what that's about. For Chrissakes, don't fuck with her."

I looked at his face, studying his eyes and the turn of his mouth, and then slid behind the wheel of my car, slamming the door behind me so hard and fast I nearly caught his hand.

He'd hit me below the belt because he

knew about Johnny and the way he'd died and the aching tenderness that would always be part of me, and he'd taken it—that painful confidence I'd shared when we'd meant something to each other—and was using it now to protect somebody. I just wasn't sure who.

"Don't do this to me, Brandon," I said as I shifted my car into reverse and backed out the driveway. "Don't *you* fuck with *me*."

11

"**I**'ll tell you one thing," Jake said. "Storey probably knew about you and Pike before he even walked into your office. That was why he hired you. He wasn't the kind of man to hire somebody, pay them a grand, and not know everything there is to know about her."

Jake was standing in my kitchen, getting ready to fry the oysters he'd mentioned on the phone earlier. He had taken off his charcoal gray jacket, draped it neatly across one of my kitchen chairs, and tied a towel around his waist, which wouldn't protect his shirt or the red-and-blue-striped suspenders that ran down his chest and were attached to his tailored trousers. Since neither of us was going anywhere and we hadn't eaten, he'd offered to cook. I never get oysters right; they always end up too tough or too salty or both, so I was glad when he'd offered.

"And I'll tell you something else," he

added, as he bent over to check the flame that flickered under the ancient cast-iron skillet filled with hot oil. "Why ever he said he was hiring you, you can bet that probably wasn't why he did it."

"What makes you so sure?"

"Think about it, Tam." He dredged each oyster in a mixture of cracker meal and flour preparing to fry them. Then he wiped his hands on the towel as he stood back waiting for the oil to get hot.

"Why would a man like Lincoln Storey care one way or the other about who his step-daughter was sleeping with? He had his hands full with her girlfriend, and he was the kind of dude who really didn't give a damn about anybody but himself anyway."

"What about his money?"

"There may have been that, and other reasons, too, something to do with Brandon Pike, probably . . . Maybe he had another reason for wanting you to follow Pike . . . or maybe it was Alexa he really wanted followed but for some reason didn't want to tell you."

I nodded in agreement. Jake could be right. I took a sip of wine and thought about Hillside Drive. I'd been pissed all the way home about Brandon's parting crack, which had hit me in the heart, right where he'd aimed. The quirky blend of desperation and bravado that characterized Alexa made what he'd said ring true.

161

All in all, I wasn't sure what to make of the afternoon. I hadn't known exactly what I was looking for when I'd headed up there, and I wasn't sure what I'd found. Words that come too easily usually aren't worth the air it takes to speak them, and the answers I'd gotten from mother, daughter, and even Brandon Pike had all been as smooth as an old pimp's rap.

All I knew was what they didn't mind me knowing: that Daphne and Storey had renewed their love connection, despite the other Tashas in his life, and that his financial affairs had fallen very easily into her size-4 lap. I also knew now that she was that second "witness" I'd been looking for, except she'd only "witnessed" what Jackson Tate had told her. Alexa had also confirmed that she and Tasha were friends, like Tasha said they were. And finally, courtesy of Brandon Pike, I knew that Alexa's daddy had killed himself the way my brother had.

But the truth usually lies in the unspoken, the glances that don't quite meet the eye, the anger simmering right below the surface, and of the three of them, Alexa had revealed the most between her undisguised hatred for Storey and her voice that concealed neither the contempt she held for her mother or the slavish adoration she felt for Brandon Pike.

And there were the lessons I'd learned about myself—that I'd been more wounded by slavery's residue than I wanted to admit, that my unresolved feelings about my mother were still so strong the casual scent of a fragrance could bring them back.

"The secret to frying oysters is keeping the oil hot," Jake said, breaking into my thoughts. "You've got to be fast with it, too, because oysters are fragile. It's not like frying porgies or whiting; they're very tender."

"Takes a tender brother to fry a tender oyster, huh?" I joked.

"You might say that," he said with a self-conscious grin. "Now watch." He carefully dropped three oysters into the hot oil. "You don't want to crowd them or they'll all clump together. Give them their space. You've got to respect their integrity. Let them be who they're going to be. Speaking of being who he's going to be, where's my boy?"

"He left a note about playing ball tonight. Where's Denise?" I didn't ask him about Phyllis; maybe it was guilt that prevented me, or something close to it. I didn't want to think about that part of his life now, and I felt bad about it.

But Jake had thought about it, and I could see his thoughts in the sadness that passed over his eyes.

"Denise is over Phyllis's sister's place tonight. Phyllis was having some, uh, problems, and I dropped her by the hospital earlier," he said quietly, avoiding my eyes.

We left it at that as we always did. Friends

do that for each other, not pushing the other where he doesn't want to go, accepting the silences along with the chatter. Jake and I were friends first and always so we never forced ourselves to take more steps than we were ready to handle.

"Where did you learn to fry oysters?" I asked after a minute.

"Jackson Tate."

"Jackson Tate?"

"When I worked for him while I was in school."

"I didn't know you helped him cook, too."

"He knew I liked to cook, so occasionally he'd show me the tricks of the trade, as he called them. Jackson and I got to be pretty tight. We'd talk a lot—about the past, about the city and where it was going, which was why I was so angry when he left town. Seemed like he was betraying everything he believed in."

"He and my daddy were good friends, too. In the old days. I wonder if Jackson knew Lincoln Storey back then. They all grew up around the same area. Daddy said Storey was a battered kid."

"Lincoln Storey? Jackson never mentioned him. Not that he would necessarily. So Storey was an abused child?"

"It's funny that I remembered it," I said as I got out a plate for him to drain the oysters on. "About Lincoln Storey. But when daddy mentioned it, it left an impression. Hitting a kid was something so far out of my experience; what daddies were supposed to do was tease or play checkers when they weren't too tired. Mothers were the ones who hit you. Isn't that something?"

Jake just shook his head sympathetically without saying anything about it one way or the other. He knew what I was talking about and he let it alone the same way I let the stuff with Phyllis alone.

"That was probably why it stuck," I continued. "Grown men got drunk on Friday nights, maybe, but they didn't hit their kids."

Jake carefully placed the first oysters on the plate and added some more to the frying pan, stepping back from the popping grease.

"Maybe we should have started another pan going. I'm liable to be here frying these things all night."

"You asking for help?"

He shook his head. "No, sounds like your day was worse than mine; just relax and enjoy it. But I didn't realize your daddy and Jackson grew up together," he added after a pause. "Jackson is one of those dudes who'll sit down over a bottle of scotch and tell you all his business one night, and then barely say hello the next. He keeps to himself a lot. Did you know he has a kid?"

"A child? Was he married?"

"I don't know. He may have been. He didn't

mention a wife, though. We were shooting the bull one night, and when I started talking about Denise he mentioned his kid. I got the impression it was a boy. I got the feeling there was bad blood between him and the kid's mother, and she never let him see him."

"Papa was a rolling stone, eh?"

"That's the way it seemed. But who am I to say? For all I know, he may have lost contact with her and the kid when he was in jail."

"Jackson was in jail?"

"I thought you said you knew the man."

"I didn't know that. My father never mentioned it, anyway. What was he in jail for?"

"Manslaughter." Jake took out another bunch of oysters.

"Manslaughter! No wonder daddy never mentioned it."

"He was young when it happened. We were talking one night, closing up the place. He kept saying that he was proud of me for doing something with my life when I was young, not wasting it like he had."

"How long was he in for?"

"A good ten years. Got out on parole for good behavior. He wouldn't get away with that kind of time now."

"Who did he kill?"

"He never went into that. Some dude the world didn't care about. Jackson got mad at him. Shot him dead. Spur-of-the-moment. Somebody trying to do him wrong. Jackson

166

always seemed like Mr. Nice Guy, baking biscuits and making gumbo and stuff, but he could get evil. The real deal was anybody who really knew him didn't cross him. And if you did it once, you sure as hell didn't do it again."

"You think he could have killed Lincoln Storey?" I asked Jake. It had struck me suddenly, the one person I hadn't let myself seriously consider. *Once a killer always a killer?* I wondered if the D.A. knew about Jackson's record. Would I have to get Tasha off by tossing them Jackson Tate? Just thinking about it made me sick.

"Kill Lincoln Storey? Jackson Tate? No, no way."

"Why?"

"Because he had a record, Tam. Because he had too much going for him. He'd put it all behind him. He'd told me once that everything he'd done in his life was to make up for that, and despite that temper he is really one of the most gentle brothers I've ever known. Most folks didn't even know that he'd been in jail, and that was the way he liked it. I must be one of the few people around that knows about him."

Could that have been what Lincoln Storey had on Jackson Tate?

I couldn't imagine Jackson's face distorted into the kind of rage that it takes to kill somebody. Or maybe there had been no distortion, just the kind, pleasant demeanor I'd known all my life. Both possibilities made me shudder.

Jake had picked up some coleslaw and a loaf of French bread at the store. We both grabbed plates and sat down across from each other at the kitchen table. It felt strange sitting across from him, and we avoided each other's eyes for a moment as we ate in silence.

"They're good," I said finally, surprised at how crisp and tender they were.

Jake looked up then and smiled, and I smiled back, both of us suddenly at ease.

We ate for a few minutes, me trying not to obviously eyeball the remaining oysters on the plate and stuff more than one in my mouth at the same time.

"You know, Jake, I was there. I keep feeling that I'm missing something. If I can establish who did what when, I can establish who had the opportunity, forget about the motive for a minute. That doesn't come sometimes until you know who did it." I remembered the last big case I'd had and a murderer named after a summer's month.

I took my black and white notebook out of my pocketbook, tore out a page, and wrote 8:30, which was when I'd gotten into Tate's, way before 9:00 like Storey had asked me to. Then I scribbled down the names and approximate times that people had entered and exited it above and below it.

- Night before—Jackson Tate tests recipes

- 6:00   Tasha arrives to set up things

- 7:00   Lincoln arrives and fights with Tasha

- 8:00   Stella Pharr arrives

- 8:30   Me

- 8:50   Jackson and I go into kitchen. Meet Storey and Stella Pharr. Tasha comes in

- 9:00   The Storeys and Brandon Pike arrive

- 9:35   I overhear Daphne and Alexa in ladies' room

- 10:15   Storey drops dead

I shoved the paper over to Jake so he could take a look, and he read it over carefully.

"So where was the bean dip?"

"Tasha brought it in when she came around 6:00, put it in the refrigerator, and took it out when we were in the kitchen, after she saw Storey," I said, remembering the rage with which Tasha had slammed the bowl of dip onto the counter.

I also remembered that Tasha had been in the kitchen when I was on my way to the ladies' room. I jotted that down at 9:25, right before I overheard Daphne and Alexa at around 9:35.

"The cops are saying that Tasha put the peanut butter into the bean dip when she made it, knowing it would kill him. I know you don't want to believe that?"

"Right."

"Then the peanut butter must have been put in while it was sitting in the kitchen, which could point the finger at just about anybody."

"Must have been after 9:00, between 9:00 and around 10:00, before Storey died. That's a long span of time. Me and Jackson went into the kitchen about quarter to nine. I remember thinking how late it was getting and wondering why Brandon hadn't come yet. It was about nine when they came. Tate and I left the kitchen together right before Brandon and the Storeys walked in.

"The only other person who was in there, besides me, Tasha, and Tate, was Stella Pharr, and she was with Storey," I said thinking back. "But she might have been there earlier for all I know," I said, still trying to remember anything out of the ordinary. "Or later. But she was the one who told the cops to take the samples of the bean dip from Storey's plate."

"Maybe she knew there was peanut butter in it, which was why she told them to take it. God, I don't believe I'm sitting up here talking about that woman killing somebody. I work with the sister every day." He shook his head in disbelief.

"What's she like?"

"Stella? Very sharp. Very serious. What you see is what you get."

"I don't think she'd do it. Why would she kill her ticket to the state assembly?"

"I don't know, but you never know what's behind those layers until you start to peel them," Jake said philosophically. "So Jackson Tate was with you after you left the kitchen?"

"Yeah."

"And you didn't see anybody go back?"

"No. There was such a mob scene that night, anybody or their mama could have ducked in, mixed the peanut butter with the dip, and ducked back out. The kitchen was right beside the rest rooms, so anybody could go in there without being noticed."

"So somebody must have put it in between 9:00, when you and Tate left the kitchen and 10:00, when Tasha served that last bit of bean dip to Storey."

"Well, Tasha was in there at 9:30, like I mentioned."

"Just what you need, huh? Tasha being the last person in that kitchen," Jake said with a sympathetic grin.

I nodded in grim agreement.

Just what I needed.

Neither of us said too much as we cleaned up. When Jamal came bounding in around eight, I had a flash of guilt as I realized we hadn't saved him any oysters, but I ordered him a Dominoes pizza, which he gobbled up. Jake and I didn't talk much more about the case. I'd decided not to mention the black Honda—there was nothing he could do about it, and it was getting too easy for me to depend upon him and for him to worry about me. And I hadn't seen it again, anyway. Maybe it had been some kids trying to scare me or steal my car.

But despite the good time and food I'd shared with Jake, I had a vague sense of anxiety when I went to bed that night. When I woke up around three, the house quiet, my imagination running wild, I blamed pigging out on fried oysters for my discomfort. I got up and munched a couple of Tums like candy and crawled back into bed. But I couldn't shake the sense of dread that hovered over me, like some evil somebody was lurking right outside my door.

12

By the next morning, I'd managed to push down the sense of doom left over from the night before. I even waved at my next door neighbor as I was heading out the door, despite his perfect tulips. I also stopped by the Pathmark for that pound of coffee I'd been trying to buy all week, and treated myself to a couple of wholewheat donuts and a large cup of coffee from Dunkin Donuts.

I avoided glancing into the Beauty Biscuit as I headed up the stairs to my office, afraid I'd spot Wyvetta. I didn't feel like admitting my lack of progress or explaining that a week's worth of investigating—the two or three people I'd managed to talk to—probably wasn't going to crack the case. I didn't feel like seeing the desperate, scared look in her eyes when she heard that I'd have to let it go on Friday, and I didn't feel like explaining to her that she'd have to pay my fee even though I didn't have the results she wanted. Storey's check bouncing like it had meant I couldn't do anything for free—for her or anybody else. Daphne Storey had said she'd make the check good, but that meant billing her again and having her issue another one, which could take a good month before it finally cleared. I'd have to beat the bushes for some fast-paying jobs in the meantime or go into the money I was saving for Jamal's education to pay my bills. If a week was all Wyvetta could buy, a week was all I could afford to give her, and that realization hurt me to my heart.

"Damn," I cursed again, as I thought about the general condition of my financial affairs. I picked up the phone and called my answering service to check with Karen, the sister who takes my calls, to see if any potential clients had called in.

"Ms. Hayle," she purred. "How are you doing today?"

"Fine, Karen," I said, calmed by the familiar, dependable sound of her voice, and then wondering how much longer I'd be able to pay for the service until I had to get an answering machine like everybody else.

"Got anything for me?"

"Two calls came in, one right after the other, around eight-thirty this morning. One from somebody named Jackson Tate. Is that the man who used to own that restaurant Tate's that used to be over on West Market?"

"One and the same, Karen."

"I thought it was. He said something about wanting you to meet him at his restaurant at seven tonight. That place had some of the best sweet potato pie I ever had in my life, Miss Hayle. You can't find sweet potato pie like that up here no more. It was enough to make you sell your mama down the river. Whatever happened to that place?"

"Tate's? He moved, Karen. To Belvington Heights. What exactly did he say?"

"I'm sorry, Miss Hayle. I got carried away thinking about that pie. Anyway, like I said, he said to meet him at his restaurant tonight at seven. He said he had something important to tell you. Said it was something you should know about him, about Lincoln Storey. Something he should have told you when he saw you last time. Was that the rich colored man who died? That Lincoln Storey guy. I read about it in the *Star-Ledger*!"

"How did he sound?"

"Dead, I guess."

"Jackson Tate, Karen. Did Tate sound upset?"

"I don't know. I never heard the man talk before. But if I'd seen him in that restaurant when I used to get that pie, I would have told him—"

"Karen, you said I got two calls?"

"Yes, Ms. Hayle. The other call you received was from a party named Stella Pharr. She asked you to call her back." Karen, moving into her professional mode, read off Stella Pharr's work number, which I copied down.

"If you see that Jackson Tate, will you tell him—"

"Sure, Karen," I said and hung up.

But I did feel better; the messenger was definitely worth the money I paid for the message.

What did Jackson have to say about Lincoln Storey that he hadn't said before? What had changed? Would I end up tossing my father's old friend to DeLorca in exchange for Tasha Green?

I didn't even want to think about it. I made the next call quickly to take my mind off the possibility.

"Stella Pharr," she answered in her clipped, direct voice. I thought of Jake's words about getting what I saw, but what exactly was I going to see?

"Ms. Pharr, this is Tamara Hayle, returning your call."

"Ah," she said as if pleasantly surprised. "Thank you for calling me back. I understand that you have been hired by somebody to do some supplemental investigation into the murder of Lincoln Storey?"

Word was traveling fast.

"This office usually doesn't deal officially with private investigators," she said haughtily and paused. "But I have something that I think will interest you. Would it be possible for us to meet today? After work, here at my office, around six."

"Can you tell me what this is about?"

"I'd rather not say on the phone."

"Okay, six is fine."

"Thank you so much, Ms. Hayle."

"Thank you so much, Ms. Pharr," I said, realizing with sudden embarrassment that I sounded like I was mocking her. I quickly hung up, and then wondered if I should call her back and make it earlier since I'd be meeting Jackson at 7:00. But I called him back instead and left a message on his machine that I might be running late.

I turned on my computer, pulled up the file named DBBD, and scrolled down to Jackson Tate's name, where I jotted down everything that Jake had told me about him and that we were meeting today at 7:00. I also made a note that I would be meeting Stella Pharr and added three question marks after her name— three seeming as good a number as any. I recalled when I'd last seen her, huddled cozily with Storey at Tate's that night. I also thought about DeLorca's comment, which had puzzled me. I wished now that I'd questioned him about it.

". . . for reasons of her own that will remain her own, was watching the wife like a hawk that night . . ."

Had Stella been sleeping with Storey too?

My man definitely got around.

As I was jotting down questions to ask her, so I wouldn't be as unprepared as I'd been when I talked to Daphne Storey, I heard a determined knock at my door, followed by a small, unsteady voice.

"Tamara, are you there? It's me." It was Tasha Green. "I got out on bail this morning, and I need to talk to you. It's important."

I shoved my notebook back into my bag and quickly let her in.

"I guess Wyvetta got the money together."

"Yeah. She had to put the Biscuit up."

I didn't comment on that, but I knew what that meant to Wyvetta. The Biscuit was everything she had or would ever have. "How are you feeling?" I asked Tasha, noticing how different she looked this morning, more fragile than she had in jail, or maybe it was her attitude that had changed; she seemed subdued, almost shy. Or maybe it was the realization what her freedom was costing her sister.

"I'm okay."

"You don't look okay."

"It's really costing me to have this baby," she said.

"Costing you? I thought you were going to be the one to get paid," I said, annoyed as hell, but deciding to treat her response like she was joking.

But she wasn't. She looked at me like she

178

wanted to hit me and then her eyes dropped down to her left wrist, which she started to rub. "Everything is hurting me. That's what sickle-cell anemia does to you. Everything hurts when you have a crisis."

I didn't know a lot about sickle-cell anemia, except that if you had the disease it could be a bitch. Tasha looked like something was royally kicking her behind.

She was dressed in loose Girbaud jeans and an oversize red crewneck sweater pulled down low, which hid any hint of pregnancy. The brightness of her sweater made her skin look pale and pinched. She hadn't bothered to put on earrings, and the double holes formed tiny dark circles like punctures in each ear. Her short black hair was brushed straight back, like a porcupine's. She looked small, weak, and scared.

"I've been sick," she said, confirming what I suspected. "It comes that way when it comes. I get pains in my back, in my joints. If I get too tired or get dehydrated. Being in that damn jail could have killed me, Tamara. I don't even know if I can carry this baby to term."

"Do you want to carry it to term? I got the impression last time we talked that all you cared about was the money." A pained look came across Tasha's face, and for a moment I was sorry I'd brought it up.

"It's a done deal," she said sharply, without

further explanation, reminding me that Tasha was tougher than she looked. I leaned back in my chair and studied her for a minute, not saying anything, wondering what she was up to.

Her face softened suddenly. "But the truth of it is, this baby is the end of my family. It's a little bit of me and Wyvetta and mama and daddy, besides Lincoln Storey. So I want this baby to live.

"You know that's what mama died of," she added after a minute.

"Sickle-cell anemia?"

She nodded that I was right. "They didn't know much about it back then. It could kill you before you were forty. Having me as late as she did probably made her sicker. But it's different now. As long as you take care of yourself." She looked away from me, over my head, out the window. "I've been thinking a lot about her. About mama, Wyvetta, about how I've let them down."

I didn't say anything to that; no need to make the girl feel worse than she was feeling.

"Tasha, I know you didn't come here to talk to me about your mother and your illness," I finally said gently. "Why don't you tell me what's on your mind."

"If I go to jail for killing Lincoln, I'll never get out," she said quietly. "If I go to jail, this shit will kill me."

"That's a possibility," I said solemnly because she was right. "They don't care a lot about chronic illnesses in prison."

"I've been thinking about a lot of things."

"The possibility of going to jail will do that for you."

"I mean, about what happened to Lincoln, about who could have done it," she said as if she hadn't heard me. "Because I didn't do it, Tamara. I've done a lot of things that I'm not proud of, but I wouldn't kill somebody."

"Not even by accident?" I asked, tossing it out just for the hell of it, my little scenario of the spoiled kid doing dirty tricks. But I wasn't even sure of that myself anymore.

"You don't think much of me do you, Tamara?" she asked as if she really wanted to know. "I mean, you don't respect me, do you?"

"I don't think you've been leveling with me, if that's what you mean," I answered her with the truth. "No, Tasha, I don't respect any woman who protects a man who doesn't give a shit about her like I think you're protecting somebody. And I don't respect a woman who has a man's baby because she wants to make some extra cash."

I let that settle in for a minute, watching the tears form and the mouth fall, watching the eyes drop down in shame. "Who is that something on the side," I asked in a low, confidential voice as soon as I knew it had settled good.

"Alexa Storey," she said. She kept her eyes on me, watching me close as she let that one settle.

"You and Alexa Storey were lovers?"

"Yes," Tasha said quietly.

"So Alexa was that little something on the side that meant something to you?"

"Yes."

"But you were involved with Storey, too, and she is still involved with Brandon Pike."

"Yes. Can I have something to drink?" she asked in the same breath.

I got up quickly, glad to be doing something, and plugged the electric kettle in. Then I set Moonlight Mint herbal tea bags into two cups, and we sat to wait for the water to boil. Neither of us said anything at first. Then Tasha's lips curled into a wry smile as I handed her the tea. I thought about the last time we'd talked about her love life, about her affair with Lincoln Storey and the fast talking B-girl bravado that had marked that tale. This was a new Tasha, one stripped down to the core. I poured the water, and we waited for the bags to steep, both of us watching them like we expected them to add something to the conversation, and then she began to talk.

"I haven't been involved with a woman before or since Alexa, so I don't know if that makes me gay," she said and gave a devil may care snort. "But I haven't been involved with a man since Lincoln, so I don't know if that makes me straight, either. I think I'm going to give up on sex altogether after I have this baby, be like celibate. It's too confusing." She added it like a joke, and I smiled like I took it that way, but I watched her for the nuances that would tell me she was telling it straight. She took a sip of tea, drew back like it was too hot, then studied me over the top of her cup.

"We met in New York. In Soho. Club Redemption down on Cleveland Street. They do a lot of reggae there, and we're both into it. We had both just turned eighteen. We got to talking in the bathroom, and found out we lived in the same town." She glanced down at the tea. "In Jersey, anyway. Same state. She never made a big thing about living in the Heights. I had just gotten my license then, and this guy she was with got drunk, and she didn't want to ride with him, so I ended up bringing her home. It was no big thing, at first. We were friends. We're still friends." She added it quickly, defensively.

"When did it become something else?"

She stared out the window as if she needed to look away to remember. "I guess we both just saw ourselves in each other's souls," she said after a minute. "We were friends, and then we were lovers and then we were friends and then we were lovers. We could never make up our minds about each other. Do you know what I mean?''

I nodded that I did, lying at first, and then I thought about Jake and our relationship and how it defied anybody's easy definition, even my own. I realized I knew exactly what she meant.

"I was more sure of it than she was, though. Our relationship. Understanding that there was nothing wrong with it. She's weak, Tamara. She's not as strong as me. I guess I have Wyvetta to thank for that, being able to stand up for myself, claim myself. But Alexa was ashamed of the love we felt for each other.''

Her eyes shifted away from mine and then back, her pain clearly written on her face.

"A lot of people have a problem with women like me,'' she said quietly. I could tell she was fishing for my opinion and some judgment of her relationship with Alexa.

"Tasha, I would never judge you or anybody else for loving who they love. I'm not that kind of person. Your loving is your business, not mine. Love is so precious and rare, you're just lucky you found it. Don't let anyone make you ashamed of loving somebody else,'' I said to reassure her.

"How do you think Wyvetta will feel about it?'' she asked scared, not looking in my face.

"Give your sister some credit, Tasha,'' I said more sharply than I meant to. "But what did Lincoln Storey think about your relationship with his stepdaughter? Did he know that you two were together?"

I was remembering what Jake had said when I asked. Could he have been wanting his stepdaughter followed to see if it led to his own girlfriend?

"I don't know if he knew, or if he would have cared if he had. He probably would have thought it was irrelevant, since a man wasn't involved. Female stuff, no importance to him."

"What about Daphne Storey?"

"Alexa never shared anything about her life that was important to her with her mother as far as I know," Tasha said simply. "I don't know if she knew or not. Do you know about her family? What happened to her father?"

"That he killed himself?"

"Alexa claims her mother drove him to it. That he got depressed, just like she does, and that her mother just picked at him and picked at him until he lost it. Like Alexa does sometimes. Her mother, Mrs. Storey, is truly a piece of work."

"What do you mean?"

"I mean nobody knows what drives her. Money more than anything else, I guess. Money and stupid shit, shallow shit, the kind of stuff that you think somebody like her would have outgrown by now. That's what

Alexa says, anyway. Since she's her daughter, I guess she knows.

"I guess everybody thinks their parents are truly fucked up in one way or another, but she is really over the top. Miss Daphne is always putting Alexa through major changes: Alexa is not smart enough. Alexa is not pretty enough. Alexa doesn't have any style. Everything. Sometimes I think she hates Alexa. Do mothers ever hate their daughters?" she asked as if she expected me to know.

I shrugged because it hurt too much to answer.

"And then there was Lincoln and his shit."

"What did he do to her?" I asked, suddenly remembering the shadow over Alexa's eyes when we'd talked about her stepfather. "Did he molest her?"

"It never went that far, I don't think, not physically anyway, but there was a kind of leering way he had of looking at her. Suggestive shit he would say to her. It made her put her whole womanhood thing on hold for a while. It made her depressed. It also made her hate him, and hate her mother for putting up with him. She got so depressed—" Tasha stopped short then, but Brandon had already filled in the blanks.

"I knew how she felt, though."

"About suicide?"

"No, not that"—she looked up surprised—

"but I get depressed about my life. Sometimes I feel like I won't make fifty."

"Why did you get involved with Lincoln Storey, knowing what you knew about him, knowing how he was with his stepdaughter?" I couldn't hide my disgust about that.

"It was the money," Tasha said, with a halt smile followed by a sigh. "And the fact that I was curious, too. I'd only had one other man, this guy in high school, and we did it so quick, listening for his mother to come home, that I hardly felt it. I wasn't sure if I was gay or straight or bi or what. Lincoln seemed as good a way to find out as any.

"And then Alexa was involved with somebody else then, too. Some white boy with a lot of money, who liked the fact that he was doing a black chick. She slept with him just to prove that she could do it because she didn't want to accept our love.

"And Lincoln was really trying to kick it to me by then. I think sometimes he did everything to me that he really wanted to do to Alexa." She stopped abruptly when she said this, as if surprised by her own revelation.

"You know I was involved with that man for almost four years. I think about our relationship now"—she shook her head as if she were disgusted—"I feel like—you know, I was twenty and he was in his fifties. I didn't kill him, but I should have."

"You were old enough to know better. To

say no, if you wanted too," I said, not wanting her to push this victim thing too far. "You got something for it, Tasha. You also betrayed the love you felt for Alexa."

"She betrayed me first."

"With Brandon Pike?"

"He's the latest, the last straw." A look of contempt came and left her face. "She felt like he was it. The one. The man. The great love of her life. The big beautiful stud who would stroke away any feeling that was left between us with his long, hard dick. Maybe she was right. He seemed to give her something that she needed. It scares me how much faith she put in that fool, how much of her is tied up with who he thinks she is."

But that was Brandon's special talent, giving women what they thought they needed.

"Is there anything between you and Alexa now?"

"I guess there always will be, something. She would never admit it, though. But I do. It went deeper than anything I've ever had. It is the one true thing in my life."

"And Alexa was there when her stepfather had that first reaction?" I asked despite it.

"Yeah."

"You said before she came to return something, to give you back something that night, something you had given her. What was it?"

"A ring. It had belonged to my mother.

That's why she came into the kitchen. When she had it, we both knew that despite the men, we had something between us that nobody could touch." She paused for a moment. "To give me back my ring, it really ended things. It hurt me when she did it." She slumped back in her chair then, and put the empty cup back on the desk.

"Remember last Monday you said that two people had talked to the cops about what I'd said that day? Was one of them Alexa?" she asked, her voice suddenly anxious. "Did Alexa tell the cops that I had said that mess about Lincoln? Did Alexa try to make it seem like I had done it?"

"You think Alexa killed him, don't you?" I said without answering her. "That maybe he crossed some line with her, maybe did some unspeakable something that pushed her over the edge. Maybe she decided that she needed Lincoln Storey's money as much as her mother did, and she didn't want to chance something happening to take it away—like staying with Brandon against Storey's wishes. Maybe Storey cared more about your relationship with her than you thought—enough to make sure she never saw any of his money. Or maybe she just got sick and tired of him and the way he treated people she cared about, maybe she just had that much rage. You think she killed him?"

Tasha stared up at where her eyes had been

earlier, avoiding mine, looking out toward somewhere above my head.

"I just know that I didn't kill him," she said in a tired, small voice after a minute. "And I know I don't want to die in jail for something somebody else did. There ain't that much love in the world."

13

Flanked on either side by file folders, three law books, and several yellow pads, Stella Pharr sat very straight behind her sturdy oak desk. Her office was compact and neat, as efficiently put together as the person who lived there. As I sat across from her, that's what I sensed that she did—save a couple of hours at night or in the early morning when she finally dragged herself home, this office was where Stella Pharr could be found. There were no photographs on the desk or on top of the gray steel file cabinet that stood against the wall, no comical drinking mug revealing its owner's sense of humor, or brightly colored seat pillow challenging the institutional flavor of the place.

There was, however, a large, gaudy star made of gold foil sitting on top of her computer that immediately caught my eye. It was the kind of cheap ornament you see perched on top of a fake Christmas tree in a liquor store, about as out of place in this office as a cut-to-the-crotch mini and pair of black fishnets. Stella Pharr's eyes followed mine to the star, and then returned to the open folder in front of her, offering no explanation or discussion about it. I sat up straight like I used to do in school when the teacher barked out attendance.

She was dressed in a smartly tailored chocolate brown suit that looked like she'd gotten it at Barney's and paid full price for it. Tiny pearl post earrings graced each ear, complemented by a dainty Piaget watch on her thin wrist. The French twist that had pulled her face tight last Friday was still on duty, and a pair of tortoise-shell glasses rode the top of her head like a crown. She wore Shalimar, which had become my "signature" fragrance in high school. It had been a birthday gift from Randy, my lock-picking first love. Johnny claimed he'd swiped it from the fragrance counter at Bamberger's. It had seemed a sophisticated gift to a seventeen-year-old— the most extravagant gift I'd ever gotten from a boy, and the whiff of it brought back our shy, passionate love-making—two kids trying to be grown too fast. It seemed too young and innocent for this hard-as-nails environment, like that gold star, a curious bump in a smooth exterior. Because Stella Pharr was lawyer-perfect, even though you sensed she'd freeze-dry your hand if you shook hers. Definitely the kind of closed-mouthed, serious-minded sister you'd want sharing attorney-client privileges if you were up for Murder One, or the kind who'd go for a public hanging if she were on the other side. I've always been slightly in awe of women like Stella Pharr, and a little bit envious. She'd never have to sweat a check clearing or dip into her kid's college fund to pay the electric bill. She looked like she had it all together. I had to hand it to the lady.

"Thank you so much for coming," she said, her dark eyes not leaving mine. I'd noticed those eyes when I'd met her that first time with Jake, and then again with Storey. They were the kind of eyes that wouldn't leave your face until they got what they wanted, one way or the other. She removed two sets of photographs. She examined each set and then handed them to me. I took them without looking at them.

"Let me get to the point, Ms. Hayle. When I called to ask Roscoe DeLorca—I think you know who he is—what kind of progress he was making on the Storey murder case, he mentioned that you were working on it. He seems to have a lot of respect for you," she added as an aside. Her tone failed to reveal if she agreed with his opinion or was surprised by it. "He's sure that he's arrested the right person, but I'm not convinced, and I want to make sure every base is covered. For example, I know for a fact that Lincoln Storey had replaced that kit of adrenaline after he'd used it during that first allergic reaction, because he mentioned to me that he'd bought a new one. He replaced it right after that first attack." She paused for a moment, watching me closely to see if I was taking it in. "And I thought you might be interested in those," she added, nodding toward the photographs. Then she sat back and crossed her arms in front of her chest as I began to look through the photographs she'd handed me.

The first set of pictures was glossy as if taken by a professional photographer, and featured three young men, kids really, baggy jeans riding the waistbands of their Tommy Hilfiger underwear, caps pulled down over their thin faces; the tired, sad eyes of broken men peering from the faces of boys. In one shot, they leaned lazily on a car, as if they had nothing better to do with their time and lives. In another, they gave some unseen somebody the finger. As I studied them I realized the photos were stills from Brandon Pike's documentary *Slangin' Rock.* These were the young dealers that everybody had talked about. He'd managed to capture their desperate in-your-face machismo as well as their touch-your-heart vulnerability. Boys trying to be men in the only way they knew how.

"Now look at the other ones and then read

the confession in the folder," Stella Pharr said, an eager, impatient edge in her voice as she tried to read my feelings from my face.

These photos were mug shots taken from the front and side, and the kids' faces were now void of expression, the eyes dead and flat.

"Now read the confession," she urged again, and I picked it up and read it.

It was long and rambling, a kid's voice using slang expressions and words. Most of it was details about the network they'd set up, who they dealt for, where they dealt, how they'd gotten the drugs. But I knew when I got to the last two pages what she wanted me to find.

They had been picked up at a basketball court by Brandon Pike, who had hired them to pose as young cocaine dealers in his film. He'd coached them on what to wear, what to say, how to act, how to fit the public stereotype of the look and sound of a dealer—somebody's fantasy of young black men gone wrong. But the fantasy had eventually become reality for them. Brandon Pike had helped the process along.

"There was nothing illegal in what Pike did," explained Stella Pharr. "He didn't give them the dope to deal or sell it to them or try to convince them to sell it. They were paid actors. But they were kids. He was morally responsible. He corrupted them in a strange kind of way. And as for his doc—"

"Documentaries are based on fact not fiction. They're like newspapers. You're not supposed to pay actors unless you state it in the film." I said this almost by rote, repeating what Brandon himself had told me once, when I'd been interested in such things.

"Paying a couple of kids to act in a film is not illegal," repeated Stella Pharr. "But his film, his 'real-life documentary,' was a fraud."

"What are you going to do about it?" I asked her, handing the photographs back, sickened by them and thinking about my son and how hungry young fatherless boys are for any man—be it dealer, hustler, or a Brandon Pike—who will offer them what they think their mothers can't.

"There wasn't much I could do. File something with the group that gave him the prize. Try to get him on fraud. But Lincoln Storey was definitely going to do something about it. He had influence and contacts and he had Pike good, and Pike knew it. Lincoln liked nothing better than grinding somebody into the ground when he had something on them." She said it with admiration, as if this were a virtue rather than a flaw, and I realized at that moment the color of the cloth she and Storey were both cut from.

But then suddenly her bottom lip quivered.

She bit it so hard I could see for a second the pale imprint of her teeth.

"Who knew about it besides Brandon Pike? His girlfriend Alexa Storey?"

"Daphne did. She may have told Alexa."

"You think Brandon Pike had something to do with Lincoln Storey's death?" I asked, putting the unspoken out there.

"I honestly don't know."

"Daphne Storey didn't seem to hold anything against him," I said more to myself than to her, remembering the warmth of her greeting and the welcome arms that had embraced him when he'd bent to kiss her on the cheek when I'd last seen them.

"When did you see them together?" Stella Pharr asked, her interest clearly piqued.

"I interviewed Mrs. Storey and her daughter several days ago."

"And how is the grieving widow doing?"

"She's doing as well as can be expected. I guess she's quite wealthy now. But frankly, it surprised me that she wasn't more of a suspect."

Stella Pharr pulled back from her desk, watching me closely, and then gave an ugly, surprising snort.

"Oh, she was," she said evenly. "She was definitely that."

"DeLorca mentioned that all of her movements had been accounted for that night."

Stella Pharr, for reasons of her own that will

remain her own, was watching the wife like a hawk . . .

"Every second." She spit the words out as if they burned her tongue. "Yeah, Mrs. Storey is quite rich now, and richer still when all the deals are done."

She got up then as if to usher me out. I didn't move, even though I knew she wouldn't tell me any more than she wanted me to know.

"Deals?"

"Selling off the assets. That's how I got to know Lincoln Storey. How we first became acquainted. I sometimes do consulting on the side, nothing to do with this office, just advice. God knows, Lincoln Storey had more lawyers than one man needed in a lifetime." She offered the explanation quickly.

"He was selling off his assets?" I asked, not letting it drop.

"One asset, anyway." She hesitated as if wondering if mentioning this simple fact was a betrayal of a client, and then deciding that it wasn't. "Tate's," she said finally. "He'd made contact with a large restaurant firm—Olsen's Taverns—who were interested in Tate's building in Belvington Heights. They had made an offer to buy it. Lincoln had decided to take it."

"He was selling Jackson Tate's restaurant to something called Olsen's Taverns?" I couldn't have been more surprised.

"The price was good, and Lincoln was always a businessman first. You sound shocked. Are you a friend of Jackson Tate's?"

"I've known him since I was a kid."

"I see." She paused, then shrugged as if it didn't matter. "He'd pretty much bought Tate out. It was over 'cept the shoutin', as my mother used to say. So is the widow going to sell? If she is, there are some things, some fine points, that she and her attorneys should know."

"She didn't mention Tate's restaurant to me one way or the other." I made a mental note to ask Tate about that, too. "But poor Mrs. Storey seemed so stricken by her husband's death. So stricken. To be sitting there with a husband she adored and see him die so violently, so tragically before her very eyes!" I nodded my head solemnly like a professional mourner. Somehow the cynical turn and bitterness in Stella Pharr's voice when she mentioned Daphne Storey's name hadn't surprised me. There was more here than met the eye so I'd decided to lay it on thick.

Nothing was lost on Stella Pharr, though. She scrutinized me like she was going to tell me to cut the crap, but then changed her mind.

"Yes," she said neutrally. "It was a tragedy."

"So what was he like, Lincoln Storey?" I asked, trying another tack. "Was he as mean as everybody said he was? God, I don't believe the horror stories that I've heard about him, everybody from his stepdaughter to Tasha, who is carrying his child—" I stopped there, letting it linger for a minute, watching that slight twitch in her eyes, and then I piled it on some more. "—who is carrying his child," I repeated.

"If you don't mind, Ms. Hayle," she said glancing away from me, toward the file cabinet, "I have some work to finish up. If you'd like to take those photos—I don't know what I can do with them. I can't prosecute Brandon Pike. Maybe you can use them in some way. Maybe it gave him or somebody else a motive. The cops are convinced that your client is the one they're after, so they don't want to hear it."

"You don't think she is?"

"I don't know whether she is or not. What I do know is that your client, Tasha Green, was inconsequential in Lincoln Storey's life." She said it bluntly, biting off each word.

"Inconsequential?"

"Of no importance. Irrelevant."

"I know what it means, Ms. Pharr. You know it for a fact, huh? That Tasha was inconsequential?"

She looked at me as if she were surprised that I was challenging her, and then gave me a what-the-hell look.

"Yeah. I know it for a fact," she said again,

irritably, as she began picking up the law books on her desk. "If you'll excuse me."

"Why did you ask the cops to check his food? What made you suspect that he'd had an allergic reaction? Everybody else assumed it was a heart attack or some kind of fit."

She looked puzzled for a minute, resting her hand tensely on top of the pile of law books she had stacked.

"I remembered his reaction that first time," she said, her eyes empty. "When the doctor was there and saved his life. It looked the same. How his body jerked itself around. It didn't look like a heart attack. I guess it was instinct, Ms. Hayle," she added in a quiet, sad voice, "the kind of instinct that's gotten me as far as it has. Lincoln always said I had it, and he was right on that, even at the end." She picked up the books now, leaving no question that our time together was over. I seized the only thing that was left to grab.

"I love that star, Ms. Pharr!" I blurted, rhyming the words together and grinning like a fool. But her response wasn't what I expected; she jumped as if I'd hit her. "Do you mind if I look at it?" I added quickly.

It was a weird, inappropriate request and she knew it, but I was playing a hunch and I held out my hand for it, not giving her time to think about saying no. She seemed suddenly vulnerable. She picked the star up and examined it herself before handing it to me.

"It's pretty. Where did you get it?"

"From a friend," she said as if she were thinking hard about something else. But something in her voice and eyes told me what I wanted to know, and I played it hard now for all it was worth.

"You were his star, weren't you, Stella? Lincoln Storey's star." I said it gently, like a teacher coaxing a scared little girl, using her first name as familiarly as if we were sisters. She glanced up, startled, and then her expression cracked. Grief clouded her eyes.

She nodded her head like a kid without saying anything, and I held the star as tenderly as she had held it, then gave it back to her. "It hurts you when people say things about him, doesn't it? Someone even told me that he sexually molested his stepdaughter. Do you think that was the truth?" Neither Alexa nor Tasha had said that exactly, but I said it now for effect. I got what I was looking for.

"That's a damned lie. That's a damned lie. I knew and loved Lincoln Storey. I knew who he was and who he wasn't."

"Would you tell me?" I gently pleaded. "Could you tell me who this man was so I can start to get this mess straight, so I can find out who really killed him." I was talking to her straight now, talking the truth, and my eyes told her that as surely as anything else I'd said. Her mouth crumbled, and then she pulled it back in shape and cleared her throat.

"My name is Star," she said, starting with something I wasn't expecting, but maybe it was the only place she could begin. "Star Farr. My mother actually named me Star Farr. My last name was spelled F-A-R-R. Star Farr. Farr Star. Can you imagine, naming a child something like that? 'See the far star shining far? Star far. Far Star.' That's what the kids used to say." She said it with a disdainful little chuckle filled with pain. "When I found out in high school that Stella means star in Latin, that's what I called myself. Stella. I changed the spelling on my last name, too. My mother hated that—said I was trying to act like I was somebody, but I was so far beyond anything she could ever dream of becoming by then, she was irrelevant." She said it bitterly with an aching sorrow that reminded me of my own.

"We were walking down 'neck' when I told Lincoln about it, down in the Ironbound, around Ferry Street. Coming back from dinner and we passed this little Portuguese bodega, it was right around Christmas. There was all this chintzy Christmas junk hanging all around—on the walls, from the ceiling—and Lincoln plucked down a star, this star, and gave it to me. 'A star for Stella,' he said, and I just started crying. 'My star,' he said. Corny, wasn't it? But nobody had ever said that to me before, and it touched me."

"Were you his star?"

"That's what he told me."

"Exactly what was he?"

"A lot of things," she answered slowly with a look somewhere between amusement and disgust. "He could be evil, there was no doubt about that. But I understood that because I've known meanness too, evil, and we understood it in each other. You don't go as far as Lincoln went, as fast as he did, without making people hate you—and they hated him. He could be a bastard, a cold-blooded bastard when he felt like it. But he told me I was the only one." She added it softly, almost begging me to believe her.

"And there was the money. There was all that money." I watched her take this in. Her lips pursed slightly as if she'd just tasted something bitter.

She looked surprised at first, and then slightly ashamed and then defiant. It was a look that said that she deserved Storey's money as much as anybody, that she had a right to it, too, just like Tasha had said it. "Yes," she said, "and there was all that money."

"Lincoln Storey had a lot of 'only ones,' didn't he?"

"Yeah. He did."

"When did you find out about the baby? Tasha's baby?"

"Lincoln told me a couple of days after she'd told him. We talked about him challenging her about it, and then we decided that

maybe we'd try to get custody. After everything was over with his wife."

"So he planned to leave Daphne."

"Yeah."

But of course.

"And he was going to get custody of this
baby from Tasha?" I asked, not concealing
my disbelief.

"He didn't have any kids. Alexa wasn't his,
and she never let him forget it. It wouldn't
have been beyond belief, him wanting to
bring up Tasha's child."

"Sounds like your fantasy, not his," I said
sharply, meaning to draw blood and wondering at that moment if this could *all* be more
fantasy than reality. "Did he tell Tasha that?"

"No. It never got that far. He wasn't all that
convinced that it was his. But he had slept
with her, even once or twice while we were
together. It didn't really bother me, though."
She sounded like she meant it.

"And it didn't bother you that he was
sleeping with another woman? A former
lover?" I said, surprised at the ease with
which she was letting me cross examine her.

"Sex wasn't the main thing between us. We
shared other things. The fact that I was a lawyer, a really good lawyer, fascinated him. He
thought that I had a future in politics—that
we could work together with that. Lincoln
liked power, and he was convinced that I
could be very powerful one day. And we

shared—'' She stopped suddenly and then continued. "I grew up like Lincoln did, poor like he was. I pulled myself up like he had. I knew who he was, and he knew me better than anybody else ever had or will. I certainly wasn't to the manor born," she added disdainfully and then picked up the star and put it back on top of her computer where it had been. "I knew she didn't mean anything to him."

"His wife or his girlfriend?"

"He had cut his ties with Tasha. The apartment. The business."

"And his wife?"

"She is a foolish, shallow woman, who depended on her looks and money to bring her everything she got. He'd outgrown her, and she knew it. She was of no more use to him."

"That's not the way Daphne Storey tells it," I said.

"Does that surprise you?" she asked, an amused glint in her eyes. "So which of us do you believe?" she asked, almost taunting me. "Who do you think is telling the truth?"

"The person who could tell me the truth is dead," I said, a sardonic parting crack before I gathered up my things and headed out the door to meet Jackson Tate.

But I was ready to bet those gold, good-luck earrings my brother Johnny had given me once that I'd find it out anyway.

14

I slipped a Miles Davis tape into the cassette player of my car as I headed to Belvington Heights for my meeting with Jackson Tate. It was the vintage Miles of "It Never Entered My Mind" and "Yesterdays," and it made me think about my father sitting in his chair sipping bourbon and remembering whatever Miles Davis brought back to him. It put me in a contemplative mood.

I can't say I was surprised by Stella Pharr's confession, but I'm enough of a cynic to know that what often passes for "true love" is usually less than it seems at first kiss. If you wanted somebody who looked like she would uphold the public trust in Trenton, Stella Pharr was definitely your girl. Storey and Stella could have taken each other anywhere either of them wanted to go. They were made for each other, and they both knew it.

Yet when I thought about it good, I had

only Stella Pharr's word for how Lincoln Storey *really* felt about her. For all I knew, that night I'd seen them talking at Tate's he could have been telling her that he had decided to stay with his loving wife.

My husband had forgiven me all my bitterness, and I'd forgiven him his infidelities.

Or so said Daphne Storey.

My girl Tasha had definitely come out of left field with her stuff, even though Alexa made more sense now. And there was Brandon Pike of the bronze BMW that didn't belong to him. I was looking forward to confronting him about *Slangin' Rock*, the thought of which stuck in the back of my throat like a piece of burnt sausage.

What could I have seen in him?

It was time for me to give that some serious thought, too. I knew his past, and he had told me things about himself that I was sure even he'd forgotten.

There was one thing I was sure of now, though. Brandon held at least one of the keys I was looking for. Jackson Tate held another.

I glanced at my watch, cursing to myself as I pulled into Tate's driveway for running so late, but I smiled when I saw his late-model black Seville. It had been my father's dream car, too—his "serious hog"—and I smiled when I remembered the excitement in his voice whenever we'd pass one on the road.

"Go on, Mr. Tate," I said out loud in praise

of the car as if he or my father were sitting beside me.

There was a red Chevrolet—looking even older than my car, I thought with smug satisfaction—parked next to it on the edge of the lot. As I drove past both cars to the back door, I wondered who it belonged to, who else could be paying Tate a call tonight. My question was answered before I got out of the car good.

The first scream was what they call blood-curdling in the movies—the kind that turns your blood and every other fluid in your body to jelly. The second came from the top of somebody's throat, hard and deep like it hurt coming out, and it stopped me dead.

Was it coming from Tate's or some kid fooling around?

There are kids in Belvington Heights who love to pull those kinds of stunts—kids with too much money and nothing better to do. I'd seen my share when I'd worked here. I stood still now, looking around me, looking for the kid.

But the screams kept coming, one after the other, from inside Tate's. I ran up the walk and through the back door, noticing that it was unlocked, and then stopped short to get my bearings.

It was quiet now, dark and still, save for the sound of my own breathing. A glow came from somewhere deep within the place.

"Mr. Tate!" I yelled. I could hear my own voice shaking. "Mr. Tate, are you in there?"

I was standing in a small storage room. I searched the wall for a light switch and then flailed my arms above my head looking for a cord, but there was nothing there. I walked a little further, feeling my way against the wall, toward the light. I realized that this room must be off from the hall that ran past the $6,000 bathrooms and the kitchen and led into the main dining room. I nearly tripped over a large can of something, bumping my knee. Pain shot through me.

I cursed out loud, and then held myself still, scared again, remembering the terror in those screams.

Who else was in here?

I went over what I had in my purse, running over what I could use as a weapon if I needed it. The only thing I could think of was a jackknife that was so old and rusty it would kill somebody from tetanus poisoning before it would cut them. No help from that. I wondered if I should go back to the car for the long screwdriver and the flashlight I keep in the trunk. But they wouldn't be worth the trip; I couldn't remember if the flashlight had batteries and a screwdriver would be about as much protection as the raggedy jackknife. I thought longingly about that .38 I keep in a box in a closet at home. Hell of a lot of good that would do me now.

"Mr. Tate?" I called out again, steadying my voice. "Are you in here?"

The light was coming from the kitchen, and I stumbled down the hall toward it. Then I heard the sobbing, as mournful and desperate as any I'd ever heard in my life, and I headed toward it.

I saw Tate's feet first, shod in expensive cordovan loafers, the tassels laying flat on either side of the shoe. One of his hands, the one with the big ring my father used to say made him look like a Tennessee hustler, was thrown across his chest, and the other was thrown above his head, the fingers spread wide like he was waving good-bye. The sobs were coming from Minnie, the maître d' who Tasha called the "hoochie." She was cradling Tate's head in her lap as if he were still alive. She glanced up at me as I entered. The brown eyes beneath the green contact lenses which made them look hazel were empty and dull.

I noticed the blood seeping through the fuzzy sweater, in the place where his heart was. The blood dripped down his sides and onto the black-and-white-checkered floor, forming a wet triangle near the hem of Minnie's black trench. Her eyes followed mine down to the blood, and then came back up to mine.

"Please help him."

I stooped down and felt for a pulse in his neck, a pulse that I knew wasn't there.

"He's gone, Minnie," I said. "Mr. Tate is gone." I said it as much to myself as to her, and I sat down on the floor beside her, letting it sink in. I started praying then, saying whatever came into my mind about Jackson and his soul.

"He's gone," Minnie said as if we were both hearing this for the first time.

"We have to call the police," I told her, wondering if she could have had anything to do with it, but I had no sense of danger from her, and my instincts about that are good; all I sensed was fear and sadness. "Did you touch anything?" I asked her gently, putting my own feelings aside, not looking at Tate or thinking about the fact that he was dead or who could have done it, thinking like a cop and talking like one because that was the only thing I could think to do.

"Did you touch anything besides his head?" I asked Minnie again.

She looked up in terror, then at Tate's body, and then back at me.

"No."

"Minnie. You're okay."

Her eyes turned grateful for my reassurance, and I helped her stand up, then seated her back down at the kitchen table. I thought about the last time I'd been here, sitting with Tate talking about Lincoln Storey over tea and a half bottle of merlot. Then I got up and went back to his body, sat down beside it, and held his hand, the one with the ring that my father used to laugh at. He was still warm, but his face had that waxy, doll-baby look that comes on twenty or thirty minutes after death. His eyes were flat, open, and unseeing. I noticed there was no gunpowder smudging on the sweater and that told me whoever had shot him had been standing at a distance, probably from the door through which I'd just come. The hole was a big one, too, definitely not a .22. I'd guess by just looking at it that it had been at least a .38.

He had been waiting for me. If I hadn't been late, he might still be alive.

I glanced at my watch, which read 7:50. He'd probably been alive at 7:00, when I was supposed to be here, when he was supposed to tell me whatever he had to say. I felt tears come to my eyes, and I covered my face for a minute, the anger so strong I didn't think I could control it.

I forced myself to get up and walk to the wall phone. My office telephone number had been scribbled on a sheet tacked beside it. I took a deep breath, as deep as I could take it in, blew it out, and then called the Belvington Heights Police Department, identifying myself and reporting that there had been a fatal shooting. Then I went back to the table and sat across from Minnie.

"Who could have done it?" she asked me like I might know.

213

I shook my head. "When did you get here?"

"About five minutes before you. I was supposed to drop off this box of papers for him yesterday morning, but my baby got sick." She pointed to a square box with a top on it that looked like a shoe box, which sat between us. "It was with my mother's stuff that I got when she died. I hadn't even gone through it. But then he called me Monday night and asked me if I had it. Mama had labeled it 'Jackson.' He had said something about closing the place up for a while, 'cause somebody had died in it and everything, and now Mr. Tate has died in it, too. Oh, Lord, life is strange." She rambled on as if she were in shock, talking more to herself than to me.

"He said he might be going away for a time. He was cashing in some bonds or stocks or something, and he wanted to do some traveling in his old age, and now the man is dead! It must have been something important to him for him to be calling me out of the blue for that box, so late at night like he did.

"I saw his car was still here, I came in and—I thought he'd had a heart attack. I thought—"

She gestured over toward Tate. "Do you think it's okay if I smoke? I feel like a cigarette."

"Let's go into another room," I said. "We shouldn't do anything in here, even light up a cigarette, until the cops have had a chance to go through the room and look for evidence."

She nodded obediently, and we headed into the dining room without saying anything else or looking back at Tate's body. I switched the lights on. The room had an eerie quiet to it.

"Two people died in this place," Minnie mumbled. She lit a cigarette, her trembling hand making the flame waver. The dark eyes behind the green contact lenses were watery. "Two people have died here in a week."

We sat there together thinking about the evil that seemed to be in the place and waiting for the Belvington Heights Police Department to show up. I felt like a cigarette, too, and I fought the desire like a champ, breathing in, then breathing out like I was smoking something.

Minnie looked at me strangely and then smiled, her lips parted like she was smiling, anyway. "I tried to give it up too," she said after a minute. "It's times like this that make me glad I didn't."

We both laughed, hushed and self-conscious, but it broke the quiet.

Gilroy came in first, her short blonde hair pushed so far under her cap you couldn't see it. She acknowledged me with a curt nod and asked me if I had been the one to call. I took her back to the kitchen to show her Tate's body, and she asked if we'd touched anything. I told her that I knew better than that, but that Minnie had been holding his head in her lap when I came in, and then admitted that I had held his hand.

"You knew him, then?" she asked me. I nodded that I had. "You shouldn't have touched him," she scolded.

"I know." She looked as if she were thinking about something that she didn't want to tell me, and then asked me to go back to Minnie in the dining room, away from the scene until the detectives had an opportunity to take our statements.

The cops talked quietly among themselves as they rushed in, but there were unanswered questions in the eyes that surveyed us, eyes that were first curious, then contemptuous, and finally indifferent. Photographs were taken, prints dusted for evidence and collected in small plastic bags. When the detectives finally got there, one smoking a cigar, and talking about a horse race in the Meadowlands, they took statements from both of us and then asked Minnie if she would mind submitting to a test, one they could give in the field, that would determine if she had shot a firearm in the last twenty-four hours. She looked at me dumbly, her eyes asking my advice, and I told her to do it because I was as curious as the cops were about what had gone down. I wanted to be sure about her, too. But there was no trace of anything on her, and I felt more relieved about that than I had about anything else that I'd learned in the last day and a half.

DeLorca came in and rolled his eyes when he spotted me.

"You again!" he mouthed. I shrugged my shoulders, letting him know with a gesture that I had no idea why I happened to be around for this kind of mess in the same god-damned place twice in less than a week. De-Lorca shook his head fast in a manner familiar to anybody who had ever worked for him, saying that he'd talk to me later.

The medical examiner swooped in finally, bundled up in a fine black overcoat like he'd just dropped by on the way to a club. He bustled into the kitchen, examined Jackson's body. Minnie and I watched them carry him out.

DeLorca came over and gestured for me to follow him to another part of the room, out of Minnie's earshot no doubt.

"A lot of shit seems to be going on in this place," DeLorca said, staring at me hard.

"Seems that way, Captain."

"You know what happened here, Hayle?"

"About as much as you do."

"What does she have to do with it?" He nodded toward Minnie.

"She worked for him."

"It could be a robbery," he said looking around suspiciously, as if he thought the perp might be lurking underneath a table. "Yeah, it could have been a robbery. Some young thug who saw the old man's Caddy sitting out there all black and pretty in that lot. Some no-account son of a bitch who decided to get some of whatever the old man had. But he looked like a tough old man, Hayle. Like he might have put up a fight. You think that's what happened?" he asked, looking at me like he expected an answer.

I didn't say anything.

"Or something else might have gone down. You think this has anything to do with Lincoln Storey's death, Hayle?"

I was thinking the same thing but didn't say so.

"Heard your client, Ms. Tasha Green, the one who did the first guy, made bail today," he said. "Did you know that?"

"Yeah," I said.

"She worked for this guy, this Jackson Tate, right? You think he knew something she didn't want anybody else to find out?"

Gilroy joined us then, a pen tucked behind her ear.

"I hear your client Tasha Green made bail."

"Maybe the two of you should sit down and talk with her lawyer," I said. She and DeLorca exchanged glances. "Are we free to go now?"

"We'll be in touch," DeLorca said by way of answering me.

It was ten-thirty by the time we finally got out of there.

"Can you give me a ride home? I don't think I can drive," Minnie asked as we walked out the door toward our cars. Her tears had done a job on her mascara. Tate's blood had dried stiff and dark on the edge of her coat. I noticed for the first time how young she looked.

"Sure. What about your car?"

"I'm going to ask my husband to come and get it later," she said. "I'll tell the cops that I'm leaving it here. I don't want to drive. I'll tell my husband to get it later." She was so distracted, she didn't know she'd said the same thing twice.

She walked over to Tate's Cadillac and touched it tenderly as if it were alive, then joined me in my car. She lit another cigarette, inhaling deeply and blowing it out in a slow, steady stream as I started the engine.

"That Miles Davis?" she asked when the tape started up. "Jackson used to listen to Miles Davis."

"He and my father," I said as I backed out of the driveway.

"Who was your father?" she asked quickly "What was his name?"

"Royal Royal Hayle. They called him Roy. Most people did, anyway. Except Mr. Tate, he called him Royal, and Daddy always called him Tate."

"Royal, like he was a king or a duke or something?"

I glanced at her out of the corner of my eye, and then realized she didn't mean any disrespect by it. "Yeah. Like a king."

"I think I remember Jackson mentioned something about somebody named something like that. I remember that name, Royal."

"They were friends way back."

"I think I remember him talking about your father. Royal."

"Really," I said, wondering how my father had come into their conversation and what Jackson had said about him. "It wouldn't surprise me."

"I'm going to miss that old man," she said, lighting another cigarette with the half-smoked butt of the previous one. "I'm going to miss that old man so much."

I turned onto the Parkway heading toward the exit closest to the street in Newark where she'd told me she lived.

It was going on 11:00 by then, and I drove without thinking, stopping when it was called for, slowing down when the guy in front of me did. But my mind wasn't on driving or even on Minnie, who sat beside me smoking her cigarette and wiping the tears that kept coming. I was thinking about Jackson Tate. For as long as I could remember, he'd been in my life with his "floating light" rolls and Christmas bourbon. My father came back to me every time I said the man's name, and now that name would be as dead as my father's. I felt numb.

What had he wanted to tell me?

Karen had been so carried away talking about his sweet potato pies, she hadn't told me what I needed to know to make sense out of any of this. Maybe it was time I bought that answering machine I'd been considering, I thought with annoyance. But it wasn't really Karen's fault. She didn't kill him.

Did he know his killer was coming to get him?

I glanced at Minnie snuffing out another cigarette.

"You okay?"

"Yeah, I'm fine. It's just a shock."

How much did Minnie know about Tate and about Tasha and Lincoln Storey? How much would she tell me? I wondered if Jackson Tate had told her anything about me.

"Do you know what I am?" I blurted out finally.

"What?" she asked alarmed, her eyes big, like she expected me to say hit woman or vampire. I had to smile despite myself.

"I'm a private investigator."

"Like on TV?" She looked relieved. A shy grin of wonder spread across her face. "I didn't know a black woman could be a private investigator."

"We can be anything we want to be these days, Minnie," I said, and then hoped that the words hadn't sounded sarcastic. The wonder in her voice had touched me, and I didn't want her to think I was making fun of her. "I mean, there's nobody holding you back from doing what you want to do anymore."

"What do you do? You know, as a private investigator."

"I find out stuff about people. Most of the time it's stuff they don't want found out."

"Sounds sneaky."

"Yeah. It is sometimes."

"You like it?"

"It's a living. I've got a kid."

"You married?"

"I was."

"I got a kid, too. But I'm still with my husband. He's in security."

"I was hired to find out who killed Lincoln Storey," I said.

"You don't think Tasha Green did it?"

"No. I'm working for her sister to find out the truth."

"I'm sure she did it," she said. "You know she is real slutty. She was going with the man, Mr. Storey, on the side. Knew the man was married, too." Minnie shook her head in disgust. "I can't stand no nasty woman like that."

"You told the cops last week what she said about Lincoln Storey?"

"How did you find that out?"

"You told them, right?"

"It was what she said. Jackson heard her the same as me. Jackson told me I should go on and tell them. Who do you think did it then, killed him?"

"Lincoln Storey or Jackson Tate?" I asked.

"Lincoln Storey."

"I know who didn't," I said. "Minnie, Jackson Tate called me this afternoon. I guess a couple of hours before he died. That was why I was there. I was supposed to meet him at seven."

"Seven?" she asked, not even trying to hide the emotion in her voice. "He was probably alive then," she said as much to herself as to me.

"Yeah," I said, my face hot with shame. "You and Jackson were close. Do you have any idea why he wanted to see me? What he could have wanted to tell me? He told my answering service that he wanted to tell me something about Lincoln Storey. Do you have any idea what it could be?"

"Oh, God—" she said as if she'd just remembered something.

I slowed the car down, shifting my eyes toward her and then back at the road. "What did he say to you?"

"Nothing." She said it too loudly, telling me with the stubborn thrust of her chin that whatever it was, nothing could pull it from her. She would not betray a confidence, even in death.

But I was as determined to get it as she was not to give it up. "What was it, Minnie?"

"Nothing," she said again, just as firmly. "It's about two streets down," she said, trying to change the subject. "Off of South Orange Avenue. A big white two-family near the corner."

"The box you were dropping off was from your mother?"

"It belonged to Jackson like I told you," she said defensively, suddenly. "Just some things he had her keep for him. Just some things he never picked up, not even after she died last year."

"You don't know what the things were? What was in the box?"

"I wouldn't open something that belonged to somebody else," she said with a sanctimonious lift of her eyebrows. Then she closed her eyes like she was praying. "It was between my mother and Jackson. Between them. It didn't include me, and I respected my mother and I respected Jackson Tate. It was just a bunch of newspaper articles, anyway. Just a bunch of legal papers that didn't mean anything to nobody nohow."

"So your mother and Jackson were good friends?" I asked, probing her for something else now, wondering how good that friendship between her mother and Tate had been.

Could Jackson Tate's "son" have been a daughter?

"Are you asking me if Mama and Jackson had something going, if they had a relationship?" she asked as if reading my thoughts. "Yeah, they used to go together, years after my daddy and her separated." She stared straight ahead again, her face betraying nothing.

"After Jackson got out of prison?"

"How did you know about that?" She looked at me now, her eyes big. "Not a lot of people knew that about him. He was real ashamed of it. I don't know why he was so ashamed of going to jail. Anybody can make a mistake. And it seems like they be putting so many men in jail these days for half of nothin', it almost don't matter to most folks one way or the other. Jackson didn't like nobody knowing he'd done some time, that was for sure. But I guess it doesn't matter too much now, does it?"

"No. I don't think it does. Jackson said you were 'kin' to him. 'Almost kin,' " I said, still pushing.

"He said that?"

"Yeah. Were you almost kin to him?" I asked her, pushing harder. "Or were you *kin* to him, Minnie? Were you his daughter?"

Minnie reared back in her seat and glared at me like I'd lost my mind.

"His daughter?" she asked, her voice getting loud. "Jackson Tate's daughter? You think I was Jackson's daughter? Who told you that lie?"

"Well—"

"What'd you say you did for a living?" she asked with a violent snatch of her weave to the front and an amused smirk on her lips. "You're looking for who killed Lincoln Storey and all you can come up with is that I'm Jackson Tate's daughter?"

"Well, I didn't mean—" I said, trying to recover some dignity.

"No, I'm not Jackson Tate's daughter," she snapped. "You must not have known Jackson very well to ask me something like that. He has—he had—a son, not a daughter. His wife upped and married some other dude while he was in jail, and she didn't even bother to tell her boy who his real father was. She didn't even let him carry his own father's name." Minnie shook her head sorrowfully, as if it distressed her just thinking about it. "Jackson and his son just started making peace with each other, just recently, after all these years."

"Who is his son?"

"Brandon Pike," said Minnie as I pulled up to the curb in front of her house. "And now somebody's going to have to tell the man that his new-found daddy is dead."

15

Blood is blood, but sometimes it's not as thick as it's supposed to be. Sometimes it's so thin it stands for nothing save the stain it leaves when it's spilled. I think about my mother when I consider the ties that *don't* bind, and anger and love so tangled you're not sure you'll ever make sense of them. I thought about her on my way to see Brandon Pike.

When Minnie said that somebody had to tell the man his daddy was dead, I knew that somebody was going to be me. I owed Jackson Tate that. But there was another reason, too, the one I thought about as I headed toward James Street, where Brandon Pike still lived. I wondered what would be in his eyes when I told him his father had been murdered.

The first time I slept with Brandon Pike, I dreamed he was a ghost, a phantom like one of those haints from the tales my grandma

227

used to scare us with. When I reached over to touch him, to caress the smooth, taut muscles in his back, my fingers had gone through him, straight to the white sheet that was twisted around him like a shroud.

I sat straight up, wide awake and scared, my body as cold as the sheet my hand had grazed in my dream. Brandon was beside me, warm and definitely alive. He opened one eye at a time, studied me curiously, and then pulled me down close to him, touching my eyelids gently with the tip of his tongue, and the dream had faded as quickly as my fear.

I'd known him only about three months then, but my decision to make love to him that night had been one of the surest I'd made. I hadn't been in a relationship in a year and a half. Worse, I hadn't met anybody who I even wanted to be in a relationship with. Everything in my life had turned to mud.

About two years before, I'd left the Belvington Heights Police Department on pride and principle and found very quickly that neither fed my kid. I'd nearly lost the home I'd inherited by default to the tax man and owed Jake so much money, the only way I'd be able to repay him would be to win the Pick-6 Lotto. But whenever I was ready to pucker up my lips to kiss DeLorca's butt to get my old job, I'd decide to give it one more day, and that turned into a week, which became a month, which eventually led me to Brandon Pike.

We met at a workshop on how to run your own business (something I sorely needed), where we'd exchanged smiles and business cards; Hayle Investigative Services, Inc. sounded more solid in conversation than it was in reality. Brandon called me the following week and asked me to lunch to discuss a proposition.

It turned out that he had some money to do a short documentary on black policemen, about the shit they put up with from both their brothers in blue and some with the same color skin. He needed to hire a technical advisor, a professional who knew her way in and out of the closed, secretive world of cops. We sealed our deal with a handshake and a glass of wine over dinner that night. Soon the dinners got longer and the wine more plentiful.

The men I'd known had all been like my father: working men who used their hands and saved their heads and hearts for church on Sunday and loving a good woman. Brandon's work was of the spirit, or so he told me. He was an artist—the first I'd ever really known—and he made me feel like that "natural woman" Aretha used to sing about. I gladly shared my knowledge, my body, and my soul. It took me longer than it should have to realize that his interest in me faded at the same rate as his need for my professional advice.

We'd talked about our families only once

that I could remember. About two months after we'd been together he met Jamal. I was surprised by his awkward unwillingness to connect in any way with my son. When I asked him about it, he told me that it was hard for him to reach out, he said, especially to a kid. His own father was dead, he'd explained, and he'd been an outsider in his stepfather's home. His mother was all he had had and she was dead, so there was always a hunger within him for something that couldn't be.

From the moment I'd met him, I'd sensed that need so similar to my own, and it had deepened after that confession. I'd been attracted to his talent, style, and unbridled ambition. But I had loved him for his vulnerability, the thing he liked least about himself.

There were no fights or resentful words when he left, no ugly scenes to peg my feelings onto, just calls not returned, dates broken without explanation, indifference and neglect—a sham of a relationship during a time in my life when I didn't need it, and he'd known that. I'd been burned by enough men to make me wary, but Brandon had made his way into my heart more easily than he should have, and he had left me bitter in ways that still frighten me.

I glanced at the clock in my car, which read 11:30, and realized I should call Jamal. I'd begun to make a big deal out of making him tell me where he was going and what time he was coming home, and I knew he worried about me when I was out late. I also wanted to tell him to spend the night at Annie's. I didn't think he was in any danger, but I didn't know what was going on or who it would touch, and if it touched me, I didn't want Jamal anywhere near it.

I pulled up to a phone booth near an all-night fish-fry place called Bensen's, and the smell of crisp fried porgies mingling with the earthy scent of collard greens simmering somewhere in the background made my stomach rumble. I called Jamal and told him I'd be late, and then called Annie and asked her to pick him up, no questions asked. Then I called Brandon, amazed that I still had his number committed to memory.

The phone rang four times before an answering machine clicked on and a tinny mechanical voice warned me that the message box was full and referred me to another number, which I realized was the one he used for business. I dug around in the bottom of my bag for another quarter and dialed that number quickly, only to be told that Mr. Pike would be out of the office until Monday morning.

I slammed down the phone in frustration, decided to go home and let the cops handle the details, then remembered that the cops knew less about Tate's surviving kin than I did. If Minnie hadn't said anything tonight, she probably wouldn't call and tell them now. Brandon would read about his father's murder in the *Star-Ledger* along with the rest of Essex County. I didn't owe Brandon shit, but I owed Jackson Tate this last one—for my father and for all those "Puddin's" and winks that had made me grin for as long as I could remember.

So I got back in my car and drove down Central Avenue, turning on to Washington Street, which James Street deadends into. I was almost there anyway. I'd decided to leave a business card with a written message on it tucked inside his door, an ironic touch since that was how we'd met in the first place.

James Street, which runs about four blocks long and is within walking distance of the Newark Museum as well as the venerable Ballantine House, had once been a neglected stretch of dusty nineteenth-century tenements in my brother's day.

"Those were some tough little brothers back when I was a kid," he used to say whenever I mentioned the place. "Them little hoodlums chased me, I mean they chased *me*, Johnny R. Hayle, home from a party one night." And then he'd howl a laugh that erupted from the bottom of his belly and exploded at the top of his head, and I'd laugh, too, and imagine my big brother, eyes bugged, coat flying behind him, running for his life for a block and a half.

That image had been James Street for me, until I met Brandon, and felt like I'd come up a notch or two along with the street. There was still an old-fashioned feel to the place, but it had been reclaimed by well-heeled lovers of the city determined to restore the area to its former glory. Brandon had been one of the first people to buy a coop there, furnishing his huge two-bedroom on the top floor of a restored brownstone with an artist's eye for style and a miser's sense for a bargain, which had impressed me as much as anything else about him. But for a fleeting moment that first time I'd stepped into his place, I wondered what had become of those kids who had chased my brother home.

As I parked, I decided the open space was a sign from God; I was doing the right thing coming to Brandon's. There was also a light shining from his top-floor apartment. I found a slightly soiled business card tucked in the photograph compartment of my wallet and scribbled a message telling him to call me, underlining the word "immediately" to emphasize my point. I crossed out my business number and wrote my home phone number on it in case his memory wasn't as sharp as mine.

The front-porch light was on, and I rang the first bell, which was marked "Tilsen." An older man with a voice that sounded like he smoked a pack or two of Marlboros a day opened the window behind the bars and peeked out. I could see the collar of what looked like a green silk robe around his neck.

"Yeah?" he called out through the bars.

"I'm sorry, Mr. Tilsen. I'm looking for Brandon Pike."

"He's not here."

"Who is it, Walter?" I heard a highly pitched woman's voice ask from inside the apartment.

"Some woman to see Pike," he yelled back.

"Tell her he's out of town."

"Brandon Pike is out of town," he said gruffly. "What do you want with him?"

"I'm Tamara Hayle. I'm a private investigator," I said quickly, not wanting to remain "some woman" any longer than necessary. I pulled another business card out of my wallet and held it up for him to see. He glanced at it and then handed it back at me.

"I can't read that thing from here," he said like it was my fault. "What do you want with Pike?"

"Some very tragic business," I said solemnly. "Concerning his family."

"Tragic? Did you say you were a cop?"

"No," I said without offering anything else.

"Why don't the police handle it?" He looked me over once again suspiciously, and asked another question before I could answer. "Why don't you call him and leave a message on his machine."

"I'm a good friend of his," I said, giving what I hoped would be a satisfactory answer to the first one. "And his answering machine was full. I wasn't able to leave a message."

"That's the problem with those damn machines. Why don't you wait till he's in?"

"It's something I think he'd want to hear from somebody he knows as soon as possible," I explained.

"Well, he's not here. What do you want me to do?"

"I'd like to leave my card with you to give to him if you will."

"You said you're an investigator. That like the police?" He paused for a moment. "He's going to be out of town for the next day or so. I think he said he'd be back Friday night."

"Is there any way that I could leave my card with you so he could get it?"

"Wait a minute." He closed the window and unlocked the front door, reaching his hand out through the crack. "Give me the card," he ordered.

I handed it to him quickly, figuring that he was going to call the number on it to check up on me. I was glad somebody from Karen's service would be there to answer. He buzzed me in after a few minutes, and met me in the hall.

"You open twenty-four hours a day? That's pretty good," he said with admiration. "Go on up to the top, that's where he stays. He might get it quicker if you leave that card for him. Me and my wife both got to make that early shift down there in South Jersey, so we got to leave up out of here 'round three in the morning. We always sleep when he get home nights. I was just about to sleep when you started ringing that damn bell."

"I'm so sorry I had to trouble you," I said, grovelling for forgiveness as I hurried up the stairs.

"Just slam this door good when you leave so it will lock. I'll tell him you came by if I see him."

I tucked the card behind the brass knocker on Brandon's door when I got upstairs, checking it to make sure that it stuck, and then headed out, closing the door hard behind me like Tilsen told me to.

It was drizzling when I got outside, and the night was hazy and had a dull chill to it. I glanced around before I got into my car, out of habit more than anything else. My mind was on picking up a whiting sandwich from that fried fish joint, and maybe adding a side of macaroni and cheese or some of those greens if they used smoked turkey instead of ham hocks. I hadn't eaten all day and my stomach was starting to feel like it.

It was then that I saw the black Honda. Rain sparkled on the sleek hood and tacky hoodlum gold trim, making it shine like somebody had just driven it out of the showroom. It was pulled into the side, about two blocks down from where I was parked like somebody had done it in a hurry, sloppily, not giving a damn.

I got in my car without taking my eyes off of it, braced for any sudden movement in front of me or behind. I drove slowly toward the Honda, straining to see through the shaded windows, but it was tough to peer through the tinted, rain-slicked glass. As far as I could tell, there was no sign of anyone inside the car or near it. I circled the block, then parked two cars behind it, wondering when and if somebody was going to come out from somewhere and climb in. Nobody came, and after about ten minutes, I got out of my car and walked over to inspect it.

I half expected the Honda to make a move for me on its own, but it remained still. There wasn't a sound anywhere on the street except for my footsteps. I noticed that the back tire close to the curb was flat. One of the front bumpers seemed loose. I kicked it twice and then again for good measure, knowing how it had gotten that way. Recalling that night that I'd been followed, I kicked the tire so hard I hurt my foot, like a kid kicking the wall in a spoiled-brat tantrum.

With the street still deserted, I went back to my car for my flashlight. I was thankful to see that the batteries were still charged when I snapped it on. I returned to the Honda and shined the beam through to the beige interior, looking for something that would tell me what I wanted to know. I spotted that something on the floor by the back seat: two tin containers, the kind that look like wheels that they use to store film. I knew then what I had suspected the minute I'd spotted the car.

"Damn you, Brandon Pike," I muttered. "Goddamn you to hell!"

I turned my flashlight off and went back to my car, calling him every filthy name I could think of. It made me sick knowing that he'd been the one trying to run me off the road that night. You never expect that kind of violence from somebody you've taken into your life. You expect it from some nameless somebody high on dope or crazy all his life, and it left me with an empty, sick feeling, like somebody had ripped something precious from me. I felt like crying for a minute; the lump in my throat was so hard I couldn't swallow. But I pushed it back down. I'd be damned if I was going to let myself cry over this.

I don't know how long I sat in my car staring at that Honda, too mad to go home and pour myself a slug of brandy and forget about it. The anger was too deep for that; it had cut a hot path right through me.

I don't usually do things that can land me in jail. I know too much about the system and how it picks its victims and victors with no justice I've ever seen. I know better than to tempt or tease the law. But it was those two things together—Jackson's death and Brandon's car—piled up on top of each other like they were—that threw me into a space I'd never been and never hope to go again.

I didn't know this man at all.

If he was low enough to try to run me off the road, he was low enough to do other things, I reasoned, things beyond the bounds of anything I wanted to think him capable of. And it was up to me now to get the truth about those things before it was too late. With flashlight in hand, I went to the trunk and got out that cigar box that used to belong to Randy.

I went back to the brownstone and rang the doorbell twice. When Tilsen opened his window, I yelled that I'd dropped my car keys somewhere on the stairs, and begged him to let me back in to look for them. He stifled a yawn, paused for a minute, and then buzzed me back in. I noisily climbed the stairs, counted to a hundred, noisily came back down and opened and slammed the door so Tilsen could hear it. Then I crept back up to Brandon's apartment, jammed open his cheap-ass lock with the shimming tool and one of the keys, and walked into his place as cool as if I'd been invited.

16

A naked bulb hanging from an old-fashioned fixture in the kitchen cast an eerie glow throughout the apartment. I turned the knob twice before I closed the door properly. I'd picked the lock easily but managed to break it in the process. I'd always heard that picking a lock is simple if you have the right touch— as sensitive as a surgeon's or a musician's. You have to get the tension just right, the pull and the push of the instruments synchronized enough to jam the lock's mechanism, "a little like humping," an old con once told me. Breaking the thing was obviously what separated me from the pros, and the momentary glow of my success as a junior lock-picker dimmed as the consequences of what I'd just done dawned on me.

I'd be the first person Tilsen would point to when Brandon told him that someone had broken into his place. Breaking and entering is a felony. I could lose my license. And for what? Clues that I wouldn't be able to share without admitting I'd been here. I'd recklessly risked everything that was important to me.

Maybe my first line of defense should be to tell Brandon (when he or the police finally confronted me) that I'd noticed the lock was broken when I dropped off my card. But Tilsen had heard the door slam when I'd "left" the second time. Even if I left now without even going into the place, I'd still be the prime suspect. I realized with a sense of desperation that maybe the only real chance I had was to find something on Brandon that would convince him not to tell the cops I'd been here.

I glanced at my watch. Midnight. The smartest thing for me to do—if there was a smart thing to do in this dumb mess I'd gotten myself into—was to lay in the cut until after three when Tilsen and his wife left for that early shift. Then I could sneak out the way I'd snuck in with whatever I could get on Brandon. But what was I looking for? I only hoped I knew it when I saw it.

The place was pretty much as I remembered. The hall was long and narrow and led to a tiny eat-in kitchen on the left, the source of the light I'd seen from the street, and then to the living room with its decorative double bay windows. The bathroom and two bedrooms, the larger of which served as Brandon's office and studio, were both toward the rear of the apartment. Each bedroom had a small closet, and there was one huge, walk-in closet between the living room and the bedrooms, where Brandon stored his winter coats and suits.

I walked past the kitchen and through the living room to the long navy leather couch in front of the window, glad that the shades were drawn. I sat down and pulled off my black pumps, jamming them toe first into my shoulder bag. The last thing I needed Tilsen to hear was the sound of my heels slapping across his ceiling. The blue and maroon antique Persian rug I'd watched Brandon charm from a wealthy widow for a couple of hundred bucks and the promise of tickets to the Sundance Film Institute when they screened one of his docs still lay in front of the couch. I wondered, with perverse curiosity, how many other women he'd made love to on its plush nap.

The oak rolltop desk that he'd stripped and finished as I'd cheered him on from my spot on the couch was still against the far wall. I tiptoed over to the bookshelves and the cabinet, which contained the TV and stereo, and leisurely scanned the various books about filmmaking and photography stacked on the shelves.

The walls had been painted a stark shade of white, which accentuated several dramatic

Dogon sculptures and the blown-up black-and-white stills from his documentaries. No shots from *Slangin' Rock*, I noticed.

The hot anger I'd felt earlier was spent now, my sense of violation dulled by my violation of him. I glanced at my watch again as I headed into the bedroom. It was 12:15. Nothing had changed in the room but its color, which was now the same bright white as the rest of the apartment. There was the same huge king-size bed we'd made love on, the same white shag rug on the floor. A blown-up photograph of Alexa Storey hung on the far wall. I stood for a moment gazing at it, struck by its power.

She looked young, little more than a teenager, and very vulnerable. Brandon had definitely captured her essence, just as he did with all of his subjects, as he had with the kids in *Slangin' Rock*. There was a melancholy longing in Alexa's eyes in this photograph, a wistful look of expectation that could only be disappointed. But the turn of her lips was what made the photograph memorable and gave it an edge. There was a smirking anger about them, a rage that bubbled just below the surface, and there was a deep sadness in those eyes that stayed with you. How often had I seen those emotions blend and erupt in murderous rage?

I looked under the bed, through the closet and drawers thoroughly and methodically but

turned up nothing. When I finished the bedroom, I went into the office, where I went
through the drawers and the datebook just as
carefully. Then finally I turned to the bathroom, envying Brandon's neatness. He had
been compulsively neat when I'd known him,
everything always put back exactly where it
belonged. At first I'd been fascinated and impressed; in the end, his fastidiousness only
annoyed the hell out of me.

It was 1:00 A.M. now. I went back into the
living room and slumped down on the leather
couch, realizing just how dead tired I was,
how I hadn't had a minute of quiet today to
review what I knew and what I didn't.

I needed more time to think, to sort things
out, get back to my computer, pull up my file,
look at my lists, take things in and try to
make sense of them the way a professional is
supposed to, not be stumbling blindly around
some ex-boyfriend's apartment looking for I
didn't know what.

When I got out of there, I decided, I would
let this whole mess settle for a day. I'd bribe
Annie to give me an alibi if the cops asked
me what I had done tonight, until I'd had a
chance to talk to Brandon. I knew I would
have to tell him about his father, but at this
point saving Brandon Pike some pain was not
high on my list.

Maybe I would run the whole thing by Jake
first, get some free legal advice, and then let

DeLorca in on my suspicions about Brandon and why I was harboring them. Although there were important pieces missing, I knew more now than I'd known yesterday. There were enough reasons to point the finger at several others besides at Tasha. And I knew one thing for sure: that Brandon Pike had assaulted me with his car either to scare or kill me. Something I could turn up here was bound to be of value to the cops. Yeah, I'd broken the law by breaking in, but the law can be stretched if you know where to pull it.

I'm not sure what made me remember Brandon's gun, the thought coming as quickly as a curse or a prayer. It hadn't been in the rolltop desk where he used to keep it. I wondered if he kept it somewhere else now or if he'd finally decided to get rid of it.

He had bought the gun, a Colt .45, because he said he liked having a gun named after the malt liquor, even though malt liquor was definitely not Brandon's style. He'd gotten it from a dealer almost as a joke. It was, after all, almost an antique, a collector's item.

That hole in Jackson Tate could have been made by a .45. But would Brandon kill his own father? I had no way of knowing what their relationship had been. Brandon had looked like he was in shock when he rammed into my car last Monday. Could it have been anger at Tate? If the gun was here, that would definitely tell me something, and if it wasn't, that would tell me something else.

I headed back toward the bedroom ready to give the place another once-over, flooded with a rush of energy at the prospect. But then I heard the last sound in the world I wanted to hear. I stopped where I stood in the middle of the room, my breath suddenly so tight in my throat I didn't think I could breathe.

"Fucking son of a bitch. Goddamn it!" Brandon cursed wildly as he stormed into his apartment, realizing that some "son of a bitch" had broken into his place. I heard him bang what sounded like a suitcase down on the floor with a thud, jiggling the lock once or twice and then kicking the door violently in anger.

In the minute and a half that he stood in his doorway calling the "son of a bitch" everything but a child of God, I darted into the walk-in closet between the bedroom and the living room, my heart pounding so hard I couldn't think. I heard him slam the door behind him with a thud as he entered the room that I'd just left.

I sank down on the floor of the closet as quietly as I could. The six long overcoats hanging there would shield me from immediate discovery. I thanked the Lord that the brother was a serious clothes horse. The smell of mothballs and old wool made me feel slightly nauseous. I closed my eyes, willing myself not to be sick. When I opened them again, I focused on the thin line of light underneath the closet door. I could hear Brandon stomping past, going toward the bathroom and then back to another part of the apartment. He was probably going from room to room to see what had been taken. How long was it going to be before he got to me? I wondered.

The telephone rang and I heard him answer it. I strained to make out the one-sided conversation.

"Yeah," Brandon said gruffly.

"Yeah. I missed the damn plane. And somebody broke in here!"

"Yeah, do you believe that shit?"

"What's wrong, baby?"

(Pause).

"Alexa, don't jump to that kind of conclusion. Alexa!"

(Long pause).

"How could you believe something like that about me?"

(Longer pause).

"Baby, calm down! Do you really think I would do something like that to you?"

"Tonight?" He sounded annoyed, alarmed.

"No, of course not. Nobody is here but me. Okay. Yeah. I'm going to have to wait to get the goddamned lock fixed anyway."

"Yeah. Ring it twice so I'll know it's you when I buzz you in."

"I'll see you."

"I love you, too."

He slammed the phone down hard into its cradle.

"That's all I need!" I heard him scream to what he assumed was his empty apartment. "That's all I fucking need. Goddamn it! Why is this shit always happening to me!"

He hurled the suitcase down on the floor then and it skittered across its surface knocking into my closet door. I froze, a chill traveling down my spine.

I knew at that moment that I had a choice. I could either stay put waiting for Brandon to open the door to find me squatting like a fool behind his smelly coats. Or I could go for broke. Throw him a curve. Stand up, walk out to confront and yell at *him* for trying to run me off the side of the road.

She who has the most gall is usually the one who walks away with the prize, and it would take some gall to walk out of the man's closet and confront him like *he* was the one who owed *me* an apology. But it was the only card I could play to get out of this mess with some dignity. And one thought blazed in my mind before everything else: I needed to get my butt out of here as soon as I could. So I played that card—slipping onto my heels, smoothing out my skirt, clearing my throat, I finally stepped out of the closet with my head held high, like I had every right in the world to be in there. Brandon was sitting on the couch, his head in his hands.

"Hello, Brandon," I said, walking toward him as casually as if I'd just run into him squeezing a grapefruit in the produce aisle of the Pathmark. He jumped up, ramming his knee against the coffee table, then cursing in pain. For a moment I thought he was going to pass out, which under the circumstances would have been the best thing I could hope for. A look of bewilderment crossed his face as he tried to fit the pieces together. With understanding came composure; it was the old Brandon before me now, as cool as a cherry ice.

"Tamara Hayle." He said my name as if it were the answer to some question. "So you're breaking and entering these days. I didn't think that was your style. I thought you had more class."

"I thought you had more class than to try to run me off the road."

"What are you talking about?" The look on his face told me he knew exactly what I was talking about. As I walked straight toward him, his expression turned from one of alarm to anxiety to puzzlement as he tried to figure what I would do next. I was acutely aware of just where the front door was and how far I'd have to go to get to it.

"You shouldn't have left your car sitting in front of your place like that. The cops know what your car looks like. They won't have any more problem finding it than I did," I said with fake confidence. It was weak, but I was banking on him not thinking straight, either.

"Breaking and entering is a felony, you should know that," he said, coming toward me now with what might have passed for a smile if I hadn't known him better. I took a step away from him, my heart beating so hard I was afraid he could hear it.

"The lock was broken when I got here, Brandon," I said, my eyes not leaving his. "I've just been here a couple of minutes. Your neighbor, Mr. Tilsen, buzzed me in. The light was on in the kitchen, I assumed you were home. I thought you were asleep or maybe something had happened to you, God forbid! So when I saw that the door was open, I walked to the back of the crib. I had no idea you weren't home. I left my card in the door, look if you want to. Thank God you're okay!

"Think about it, why would I break into your place and leave a business card in your door? I heard you out here on the phone, and I came out, but that doesn't excuse what you did to me, you lousy bastard. How could you try to run me off the goddamn road?"

My mouth was going a mile a minute, and my hands gesturing wildly as the lies and half truths flew fast and wide. Brandon studied

250

me doubtfully, his head tipped slightly to one side like somebody about to be drawn into a con. He took another step toward me.

"I guess you think I deserve this, don't you?" he said as if he really meant it. "You breaking into my place like this, accusing me of doing some shit like that."

We were facing each other now, about two feet between us. I didn't want to glance at the door, but I knew how long it would take me to get there. I also knew I would have to lunge for Brandon first, hard enough to knock him off-balance before I could make a break for it. A swift kick to the groin would do it, I figured, but I'd also forgotten how solid he was. I edged one step forward, a foot closer to the door. He stayed where he was.

"You really hate me, don't you? I can see it in your eyes every time you look at me. I guess I don't blame you, Tamara. I guess I can't blame you."

"I don't know what you're talking about."

"You know. We both know. Because I wanted it to be as real as you did."

"Oh God, Brandon. That was three years ago. That has nothing to do with anything now." I was genuinely amazed. What kind of a fool did he think I was? Was he really going to try to pull out that?

"I know you don't mean that."

"You don't know me, Brandon."

"I knew you once."

"You thought you knew me. And I thought I knew you. I thought I wanted to know you, anyway."

I added the last bit reluctantly, even though there was some truth in it. I didn't know what game he was trying to play with our past and my feelings, but I've never known a man who wanted to believe that you'd faked an orgasm or gotten over him, and Brandon was vainer than most. I was also curious.

"Brandon, what did happen between us?" It came out sounding sadder than I meant it, or maybe there was more hurt there than I wanted to admit even to myself, even after three years.

"You have no idea who I was, what a hole there was inside me," Brandon answered with a sincerity that startled me. "I did you a favor by leaving you alone, believe me." But then his eyes changed, narrowing ever so slightly, as if he'd remembered something, and he placed his hands on my shoulders, very gently. I backed away from him instinctively, but he stayed with me. I couldn't be sure whether he was truly caught up in the middle of some emotional moment or if he'd simply sensed that I was going to break for the door. But I could feel the tension in his hands, letting me know that he was in control if he wanted to be.

"I'm in over my head, Tamara," he whispered, his eyes so scared they put a chill into me. "There aren't a lot of women I could say that to, but you're one of them. I'm in over my head, and I don't know what to do about it." His voice cracked like a kid's, and his hands tightened on my shoulders. I tried to shake them off, but he wouldn't move them.

"Did you kill Lincoln Storey?" I blurted it out without thinking about the consequences, and the minute I said it I realized what a stupid thing it was to do, standing alone in there with him, with his hands on my shoulders— close enough to wring my neck.

He dropped his hands to his side suddenly, like he'd read my mind. "Whenever that old bastard had something on somebody he would never let it go. He'd torture him with it. Find a way to bring it up every time he could do it. Joke about it. Laugh about it. He was a sadist, Tamara. Do you know what that kind of shit can do to a person? How it can work you down to your bones? Make you do something you wouldn't ordinarily do?"

"Like kill a man?"

"Like kill a man."

"He knew about *Slangin' Rock*, those kids in your film, didn't he?"

"Yeah. He knew about that."

"Did you kill him?" I asked again, my fear gone now.

"I could have, Tamara, but I didn't."

There was something about the way he said it that made me remember what I'd first loved

253

about him: his well of vulnerability that had brought back my own.

"You were protecting the person who did it when you tried to run me off the road?" I asked him, knowing the answer, the only one there could be.

He wouldn't look me in the face. He looked at the ceiling first and then over my head. "I wasn't going to hurt you. It was spur-of-the-moment. I wanted to do something fast. It was stupid, just plain stupid! But I was mad and scared. I wouldn't hurt you like that. Even I haven't dropped that low."

"Just low enough to teach some kids how to deal dope?" I couldn't resist asking, but he took it on the chin without flinching.

"Yeah, baby. Just low enough to help some kids learn how to deal dope. If you forget that shit, I'll forget this." He gestured toward the front door, and its broken lock, his voice suddenly as confidential and conspiratorial as somebody telling you something nasty about a friend. "If you forget this car business, I will forget that you broke in in here. And I didn't run you off the road, Tamara. It was a couple of taps, wasn't it? If I'd wanted to run you off the road, I could have done it, but I didn't. I was scared and desperate, and haven't you ever felt like that? If you forget that, I'll forget that you broke in here tonight. Because I know you did, Tamara, and I know it would mean your license. A favor for a favor. We owe each other that. Because the thing is, Tamara, I'm not the same person I was when you knew me, or even the same one I was six months ago. Everything about me is beginning to make sense now. Everything has changed. Something has happened to me that has changed my life!"

"You sound like some hustler who just got religion. Don't go getting happy on me, Brandon, I don't think I could take it."

Anger and then hurt flashed in his eyes. "Well, fuck it then, Tamara. I don't really give a damn whether you believe me or not."

"Let's say not, but try me anyway," I said more kindly this time.

"I've been looking for him all my life," he answered.

"Jackson Tate?"

"My father."

"Storey was blackmailing Jackson about his past, wasn't he?"

"Yeah."

"And about you, about *Slangin' Rock*."

He sighed and dropped his head in shame and sadness. "Yeah, and about me too."

"And you want me to forget all this, Brandon?" I said softly. "If I forget you tried to kill me, or tap me, or whatever you want to call it, you'll forget I broke into your place. A felony for a felony for auld lang syne?"

"Tamara, don't make a mockery—"

"And we'll just let Tasha hang. Spend the rest of her natural life in jail?"

He stared at me blankly.

"Jackson told you that he killed Lincoln Storey that day that I saw you at Tate's, the day you rear-ended my car and then came back to try to scare the living hell out of me, didn't he?" I asked. "It was you who called him while I was sitting there talking to him, not Minnie like he said. He was feeling so guilty, you were afraid he was going to blurt it out to me too."

"I'd just found him, I didn't want to lose him." Brandon's eyes were filled with as much sadness as I'd ever seen. "I wanted you to stay away from him, Tamara. He's the only thing that really makes sense in my life anymore."

I paused then, wondering how I was going to tell this man that his father was dead. It took a toughness I wasn't sure I had. I sought for the words, thought of some and then discarded them. But before I could come up with something that made good sense, we both heard something that startled us. It was the sound of a key being forced into the broken lock, then the tap-tap-tap of somebody's heels as she stepped loud and fast across the hardwood floor.

17

The smell of her perfume told me who it was even before I saw her face. It was the fragrance of my mother, and the sudden memory of her cruelty sliced through me. Then it all fell into place so quickly and easily I wondered how I could have missed it.

Daphne Storey stopped short when she saw us, as surprised as we were to see her, her eyes narrowing as she tried to make sense of my presence and figure why Brandon was still in his apartment when he was supposed to be gone. And then a cunning look crossed her face, and she slipped out of the hooded gray suede coat with the poise of a woman who knows she has things under control.

"I was driving back from the city when I saw your lights on. I thought I'd chance it so I stopped by. I'm so happy you're here." She answered Brandon's question before he posed it, her eyes not leaving mine. She carefully folded her coat, placed it on the chair in front of the desk, and walked toward us. But she didn't take off the soft suede gloves that matched her coat, and she clutched her black Coach tote bag close to her body. When she reached Brandon, she took his hand in hers, closed her eyes, and kissed him gently on the lips, a kiss as familiar as it was passionate. I knew then that she had decided that I wouldn't live to tell the tale of what that kiss told, and it made me dizzy with fear.

Brandon, caught off-guard and obviously not as comfortable with the revelation of the nature of their relationship as she was, drew back slightly, his eyes still open.

"I missed the plane. Somebody broke into my place," he explained, but he looked worried.

"That somebody being Ms. Hayle?" Daphne asked, casting me a disapproving glance, like she'd just walked in on me scribbling four-letter words on the wall.

He didn't answer her, and I wondered if he believed her lie about coming to his place from New York City. But I knew the truth, and it was that she'd come back to return the .45 she'd borrowed to kill Jackson Tate. It was a truth she couldn't afford to let Brandon know. And it was the truth that might keep me alive if I played it at the moment it would do me the most good. For now, I'd hold onto it just as tightly as she was holding that totebag.

"You really are in over your head, aren't you, Brandon?" I said to him after a minute. His glance wavered for a moment. "I knew you were good, baby, but to be doing a mother and her daughter? Brandon, even for you, that must be a first, I've got to hand it to you, brother—"

"Shut up," Daphne said evenly without raising her voice.

"It was about the two of you all along, wasn't it?" I asked. "That's what Lincoln Storey was trying to get. He knew that if I followed Brandon, sooner or later he'd lead me to your bed. Then he could use that against you in any way that he needed to. But we both know it wasn't really about Brandon, was it?"

"I didn't kill my husband, if that's what you're thinking. The police accept that. Even Stella Pharr accepts that. There's no proof to tie me to his death." Daphne hesitated when she said Stella's name, which told me why Lincoln Storey had been killed when he had. I glanced at Brandon, but his face was as hard as a mask, his eyes cast down, his lips drawn tight.

"You may not have killed him, but you certainly had a hand in it, didn't you?"

"I don't know what you're talking about." She was annoyed now, and I wondered how far I could push her before she made the move she was bound to make.

"You don't know what I'm talking about." I turned to Brandon. "Have you talked to your father tonight?" I asked with an innocent smile. "Why don't you give him a call? He'd probably like to share what's happened to him."

She bucked slightly, then regained her control.

"What do you mean?" Brandon asked, his smooth, cool look turning to one of concern.

"I just left your father," Daphne said, cutting me off. "We had dinner at a new place over on 145th Street. That's where I was coming from. He said to tell you he'll call you sometime tomorrow. He wants the three of us to get together for lunch."

"What a coincidence," I said with a sly smile. "I saw Jackson earlier this evening. But he didn't say anything about meeting Brandon for lunch, or anybody else for that matter."

Brandon eyed me quizzically. Daphne's eyes narrowed as she tried to figure what I was trying to pull. The light in her hazel eyes had turned dark.

I glanced at the door down the hall, wondering if I could make it. There were two of them now, but I decided to chance it. I moved toward the door. But she moved as quickly as I did. Daphne pulled the gun out of her tote bag, smoothly, without making a sound.

"Please stop now, right where you are."

Brandon was the only one surprised to see that she was holding his .45.

"Come back to where you were standing. You're not going anywhere now."

"Where—"

"From your desk."

"What's going on, Daphne?"

"Don't you get it, Brandon? Your lady thinks she has to kill me."

"What is she talking about, Daphne?"

"You don't want him to know, do you? Not now, anyway. Not until the cops come knocking on his door," I said to her as if Brandon weren't there.

"Shut up," she snapped, and I knew by the way her eyes had changed that she meant it. She stood in front of both of us now, but the gun was pointed at me.

"Breaking and entering. We will say it was breaking and entering."

"I don't want you to kill her," Brandon said. "I don't understand why you have to kill her. I don't—"

"She who has the gun has the power, and your lady definitely has the gun, so no matter who you thought was running the show, baby, she's running it now," I interrupted him, and he backed away from her closer to me. Daphne watched him move toward me and then smiled, tipping her head to one side as if she were getting ready to tease him.

"Brandon, I'm not going to shoot you," she

said in a little girl's voice. "You know I'm not going to shoot you. It's just that she knows too much now. So you can't stop me."

"What do you know?" Brandon asked me.

"More than he knows," I said to Daphne Storey.

"What is she talking about? Daphne, what does she mean?"

"Well, let's start from the beginning of this mess, from what we all know. We know that murder always takes three things—motive, opportunity, and method. And we all know now who profited from this thing, or thought they would, who knew how it could be done, and who had the opportunity to do it because when they held the murder weapon—a cook's spoon, of all things—nobody would suspect them of anything but taking care of business.

"We all know how you can kill somebody and not actually hold a gun or hold the spoon that stirs peanut butter into somebody's bean dip, and how easily a wife can check to make sure her husband does or *doesn't* have his overcoat, his briefcase, or that little kit containing adrenaline that will save his life if he gets a taste of the one thing in this world that will take him out like a .45."

Brandon looked from me to Daphne, his voice cracking when he spoke. "You and my father were in it together."

"It's called premeditated murder," I said. "When did you and Jackson start planning it?

After you realized Lincoln was serious about Stella? I'll bet it was easy once you figured out how to do it, how easily Tate could slip into his own kitchen at a crowded party and do what he had to do, and how easy it would be to set up Tasha Green."

"She's making it up as she goes," Daphne said, but even she didn't sound convinced.

"Then why do you want to kill her?" Brandon asked, looking at Daphne as if he actually expected her to answer him.

"I had nothing to do with my husband's death," she said, her eyes big with innocence, begging him to believe her. "I love you, Brandon. I want you to be happy. Jackson killed Lincoln, just like he told you. Ask Jackson when you talk to him."

"I'd like to be a fly on the wall for that one," I said.

"The money will be ours," she said to Brandon.

"Ours?" I asked sarcastically.

"You know how much I love you, what I've sacrificed for our relationship," Daphne said, begging him. "I've betrayed my own daughter, for Chrissakes!"

"Yeah, she's really devoted to you, Brandon. After she's shot me with your gun, Brandon, who do you think they'll come looking for? How much love and money do you think you two will share once you're in jail for shooting me?"

"It will be breaking and entering. I'll testify to that. I will say that we were here together. She broke in. You shot her. Or she was here when we came in, and they'll believe me because there is nothing that money can't buy, nothing that it won't make right."

Brandon stepped toward her, and she stepped back, aiming the gun at both of us now. Was she ready, I wondered, to take that final step, to close the circle. Two murders—mine and Tate's—and a suicide—Brandon Pike's—with no trail that led back to her. Whatever money she'd given Jackson Tate—those "stocks and bonds" he'd told Minnie he was cashing in—you could be sure she'd given him in cash. Alexa would be a suspect even before Daphne would be because she stood to gain as much as her mother. And since Brandon was Alexa's boyfriend, they'd probably suspect her daughter before they suspected her.

"Give me the gun, Daphne," Brandon said suddenly, realizing just how tenuous the string that connected him to her was. "Give it to me now."

She stepped away from him, her gloved hand still tight around the grip.

And then the buzzer rang, twice, with no pause between the rings. Brandon caught his breath. Daphne's hand tightened on the gun.

"Who?" she spit out that one word, her eyes large. "Who?"

"Alexa," Brandon answered.

"Why?" she demanded to know, her eyes suddenly wide with panic.

"She called earlier. She knows about us."

"Don't answer it. She'll go away if you don't answer it. Don't go near it!"

"Are you ready to shoot all three of us? Is Lincoln Storey's money worth all that?" I asked her. She ignored me, her face a veil of tense concentration as if by sheer force of will she could wish her daughter away.

But there was another set of rings, and then Tilsen's bell sounded once, then again. There was a pause until finally a buzzer sounded loud and long as Tilsen, sick of Pike's women disturbing his sweet sleep, buzzed in whoever it was.

"She's coming up," Brandon said to Daphne, stating the obvious. He edged toward her, but she stepped away from him.

The three of us listened as Alexa bounded upstairs. She rapped hard on the door.

"Brandon?" she called out. "Brandon, are you there? Brandon?" She pushed the door open and ran into the foyer of the apartment.

"He's in here with me," Daphne Storey said to her daughter, her voice tinged with resignation. "Come here, Alexa. I have something to tell you."

18

Alexa Storey's hand flew to her mouth as if to silence a scream as she took in the scene: her scared boyfriend, me looking worse than he did, and Mama holding a .45 that was trained on both of us. As she probed our faces for answers, I noticed for the first time how delicate her fingers were, and how ugly the ragged scar was that ran across her left wrist.

"What the hell are you doing?" she finally asked.

Daphne shifted slightly, motioning with her head for her daughter to come and stand beside her. Alexa hesitated for a moment and then quickly complied.

"Your mother is getting ready to kill us," I told her. "Definitely me, probably him, maybe even you."

"Alexa, I'm going to tell you the truth, because I don't have time for anything else," Daphne Storey said. "I've always told you the truth in the end, haven't I, Alexa? Because, you know, you are the only thing that matters to me." Her words tumbled out fast, and her eyes began to shine as they welled with tears. I wondered how deeply she had to dig to come up with those tears, but then I wondered if they might be real. I thought about my son and the words I'd said to him about telling him the truth a couple of days ago, and I felt a sense of shame so deep I had to close my eyes to beat it down.

How could I have gotten myself into this? How could I be so irresponsible?

I took a deep breath and blew it out slowly, trying to calm myself down. Brandon glanced at me, annoyed, then shifted his eyes back to the mother holding the gun and the bewildered daughter standing beside her. He seemed frozen, his face immobile, his hands in fists at his side.

"I hated him as much as you did," Daphne said to her daughter.

"I don't believe you're—"

"Shut up and let me start where I have to start." The words were harsh, but her tone was more pathetic than angry.

"I hated him as much as you did, Alexa," she repeated, and that hate shone through in her eyes and was audible in her voice. "I hated him when I married him, and I hated him when he died. I hated the way he looked at you, and I hated the way he used and humiliated me."

Alexa looked at Daphne as if she knew she were lying.

"You only saw what you wanted to see when you wanted to see it, when it would do you the most good."

"He never put his hands on you."

"And if he had, would it have made a difference? Would you have done anything?"

"He was going to take it all, Alexa. Every penny of it." She glanced at her watch quickly, and then back at her daughter like she had something else on her mind.

"From the day I was born, from the day my daddy put a bullet through his brain—"

"Don't start with that!" Daphne warned. "Because you have always had, Alexa. Always. I've made sure of that. Despite how your father's lies and weakness destroyed me, I have always made sure that you would have what I had, what I grew up with."

"So you had to kill Lincoln," Alexa said, shaking her head in disgust. "You actually killed him."

"With a little help from a friend," I added.

"You said it yourself, you've been saying it for years, how he deserved to die. Don't you think I saw the way he looked at you sometimes, how much you hated him as much as I did?" Daphne continued, ignoring my comment.

"Do you know what would have happened to us if I hadn't done it? Where that would have left us? Where that would have left you?"

"Don't put this shit on me!" Alexa spit out, her eyes narrowing in anger. "Don't you dare put this I-did-it-for-my-daughter bullshit on me!"

It was the Alexa from the ladies' room that first time at Tate's, the one who had called her mother a lying bitch in her own house, and the anger flashed in Daphne's eyes the way it had that day, but she swallowed it, and when she answered her voice was calm.

"No," she said with a faint smile. "We both know better than that. I did it for me, too. Because I can't live any other way than the way I always have, the way I've been taught to. I found that out when your father died like he did. I know that about me. It's not a pretty truth, but I know it."

"Oh God—" Alexa put her hands over her face as if she was just beginning to get it. "And Brandon?" She glanced his way, acknowledging his presence for the first time. "Was he that friend she mentioned? Did he kill Lincoln? It was the two of you all the time, wasn't it? It was about you all the time?"

"No," Brandon answered quickly. "No, Alexa. I didn't kill him."

"But it is true about you and her, isn't it?"

"Alexa, I never meant to hurt you. I—"

"Damn you, Brandon," Alexa cried. "God damn you! Why would you do this to me?"

I'd said nearly the same words about Brandon in nearly the same tone of voice not six hours before. "Brandon, look around you. Here are three women. Three women! And you've done every one of us wrong!" I couldn't resist saying it to him—the one amusing aspect of this whole mess suddenly hitting me.

"Alexa, I know you won't believe me, but I care about what happens to you, me and your mother. If I'd had any idea you'd find out like this, I would have given my right arm for you not to find out about us like this." Brandon stammered a defense, not even able to finish his own sentences.

"He's not worth it," Daphne said quietly to her daughter, touching her shoulder. Alexa shook her hand off. "He was never worth it. I knew that the minute he walked into your life. That was one thing Lincoln was right about."

"So what are you going to do now?" Alexa asked her mother, drawing closer to her, as if she had finally decided what side she was on, the side with the gun.

The real question now was when was Daphne going to do it? I thought to myself. I'd guessed it that first time I'd seen her glance at her watch. She was waiting for Tilsen and his

270

wife to leave at 3:00, when the house would be empty, and nobody could hear the gun or even know when it had been shot. She glanced at her watch again as if she'd read my thoughts.

"Alexa, listen to me. I want you to leave now. Leave! It's the only way things will work out. The only chance we have." With each word her voice grew louder, more desperate. The hand that held the gun was beginning to tremble. "I've gone too far to have any other choice."

"There's another way it can go down." Brandon's eyes fastened on Daphne as his voice took on that tone that had at one point or another seduced every woman in the room. "Daphne. You know I'm not going to turn in my own father," he continued, lowering his voice as if they were alone. "It can go down like you said it could before—me coming home, shooting what I thought was a prowler, an old girlfriend, jealous, who had no business in my place in the first place, who broke in because she thought I wasn't home."

"Well I'll be goddamned!" I muttered in amazement. "You think I'm just going to stand here and let you trade your life for mine by sleazing your way back into somebody's drawers!"

"Don't let her kill me." Brandon pleaded with Alexa now. "Please don't let her kill me."

"The blood of your father is on your hands," I said, stretching out the words like some country preacher on a roll. "The blood of Jackson Tate, Brandon." I paused for emphasis, and then spit out the words that followed like they were burning my mouth. "She killed your father, Brandon. Don't you get it yet? She killed him with the gun she brought back here to return. She shot him in his restaurant tonight. She murdered your father with your own gun! Think about it, Brandon. Didn't you tell her your father's confession? That's what sealed it for him, you know. She knew then it was only a matter of time before he told somebody else."

As I watched his eyes close and his hands touch his ears like he didn't want to let in the truth, I wondered if on some level he had known it all along, if it took me saying it out loud to finally bring the truth home. He gave a shriek of grief and then rushed for Daphne, grabbing her by the shoulders, the gun be damned. She fell backwards almost at Alexa's feet, the gun crashing to the floor above her head. I saw my chance and went for it, but Alexa was there before me.

"Give me the gun, Alexa." Daphne scrambled out of Brandon's grasp and stood up quickly, extending her hand as she approached her daughter. "The worst is over now. Give the gun back to me and then leave like I told you to before." Her voice was soft, and as seductive as Brandon's had been. Alexa took a step backward.

Brandon stood up, brushed himself off, and held out his arms toward Alexa, his mouth silently forming the words, "Give it to me."

Her eyes darted first to her mother's face and then to Brandon's; contempt and then confusion came into them.

"Everyone I have ever loved has betrayed me," she said. "My father, you, Tasha, him." The words came from the bottom of her soul, and her eyes filled with the same despair I'd seen once before in somebody's eyes but hadn't known what to do about it.

"Don't," I begged as I stepped toward her, my voice coming from the place within me that I thought had died with Johnny. She studied me, her lips parting slightly as if she were trying to remember something she'd forgotten. "Please, Alexa, please don't!" She handed me the gun, then reached for my hand and held it, like a lost child does when she grabs the hand of a stranger she knows she can trust.

Epilogue

I had a lot to be thankful for as spring turned to summer that year. I was a thousand dollars and a trip to Jamaica richer, and business had never been better.

Every morning for three months going, Wyvetta Green had given me my "propers" by telling anybody who would listen how "Tamara Hayle, Private Investigator Extraordinaire," had saved her baby sister from "doom and destruction" by catching Lincoln Storey's murderer—and all in the week she'd promised. Thanks to Wyvetta's mouth, the summer was the best I'd ever had.

Jamal got a scholarship to that computer camp I'd wanted to send him to. Alexa Storey deeded Tate's restaurant to Tasha, who promptly moved it back to Newark and renamed it Tasha's after she had her son.

I'd even had the last word—or lack of it—with Brandon Pike. He'd written me a rambling ten-page letter begging me to forgive him for "those few unfortunate moments of our mutual desperation." But in the last paragraph, he asked if I'd agree to be interviewed for his new doc, *Lincoln Storey: An Intimate Portrait*, which he'd just received a grant to produce. I scribbled "return to sender" with a red Magic Marker across the top and decided to let heaven handle it. As sure as God don't like ugly, Brandon Pike will get his due.

But thoughts of Alexa and Daphne Storey stayed with me into the fall. Their bond had brought back the demons from my childhood, and I couldn't shake the lingering sadness they'd stirred up.

I ran into Alexa Storey at the Short Hills Mall as October was ending, and we stopped in Au Bon Pain for a cup of coffee. We talked for a few minutes about nothing in particular, and she told me she had moved closer to the town where Daphne would be serving her life sentence so that she could visit her more frequently.

"How were you able to forgive her?" I finally asked her.

"I had no choice. I had to find my peace. She *is* my mother, after all," she said, and then she smiled, and for the first time that I could remember, her eyes smiled with her lips.

That night I looked for those hateful letters I'd written to my own dead mother so long ago. I found them pushed to the bottom of the drawer where I keep her things: the empty bottle of Chanel, her wedding ring, the Valentine's Day cards I'd made at school and never given her. I read the letters one last time, and when no tears came, took them into the kitchen and burned them one by one in the sink.

"I love you, Mommy," I said aloud, forgiving my mother as I forgave myself, and finding some peace at last.

Explore Uncharted Terrains of Mystery
with *Anna Pigeon, Parks Ranger* by

NEVADA BARR

TRACK OF THE CAT

72164-3/$4.99 US/$5.99 Can

National parks ranger Anna Pigeon must hunt down the killer of a fellow ranger in the Southwestern wilderness—and it looks as if the trail might lead her to a two-legged beast.

A SUPERIOR DEATH

72362-X/$4.99 US/$6.99 Can

Anna must leave the serene backcountry to investigate a fresh corpse found on a submerged shipwreck at the bottom of Lake Superior—how did it get there, and, more important, who put it there?

ILL WIND

72363-8/$5.99 US/$7.99 Can

An overwhelming number of medical emergencies and two unexplained deaths transforms Colorado's Mesa Verde National Park into a murderous puzzle Anna must quickly solve.